'You made a fool of me once, Rosamund,' Nick said softly. 'You played me along to the stage where I...' Then his tone crisped. 'And then you dropped me with one single telephone call.'

'I see. You mean I beat you at your own game, and you didn't like it.'

He stared at her coldly. 'I wasn't aware at the time that it was a game.'

'Do you really expect me to believe that?' She gave a mirthless laugh. 'So this—this pitiful proposal is my come-uppance? Anyway, Ewan would be—devastated if he knew that I was repaying his debts by marrying *you*.'

Nick's smile mocked her as he lifted the latch. 'Only we two would know the truth.' He paused. 'So it's up to you. Think it over, Rosamund. On the other hand, of course, you could pray for a miracle,' he added with heavy sarcasm.

YESTERDAY'S FIRES

BY

KATE KINGSTON

MILLS & BOON LIMITED
ETON HOUSE   18-24 PARADISE ROAD
RICHMOND   SURREY   TW9 1SR

First published in Great Britain 1989 by Mills & Boon Limited

© Kate Kingston 1989

Australian copyright 1989 Philippine copyright 1989 This edition 1989

ISBN 0 263 76410 9

Set in Times Roman 10 on 11¼ pt. 01-8909-60168 C

Made and printed in Great Britain

CHAPTER ONE

'TONIGHT?' The word was no louder than a frail whisper as Roz stared at her brother. 'You mean... You said that Nick Martel—was coming *here*?' Then, in a supreme effort to control her voice, she added a little shakily, 'But I didn't realise that he was back at Meronthorpe.'

'And why should you,' Ewan said drily, 'seeing that you keep your nose screwed so closely to your own particular grindstone?'

But Roz hardly heard him, concentrating instead on trying to silence the clamour inside herself. Who would have thought, she asked herself bleakly, that even after two years the mere mention of Nick's name was enough to turn on a current that, against all reasoning, set her blood racing. She was thankful that Ewan's back was towards her, and her telltale expression went unseen.

'I assume he came back because of his father,' Ewan said indifferently. 'The old man had a stroke so ——' he shrugged thin shoulders '—the heir to Meronthorpe returns.'

It made sense, Roz thought dully, for although the relationship between Nick Martel and his father was sometimes stormy there was an undeniably close bond between them. At least, she amended, that was the way it *had* been, two years ago, when she had been foolish enough to believe that an equally strong—although different—bond linked Nick with herself.

Abruptly she stood up, lifting the coffee tray. 'Well,' she murmured, in what she hoped was an incurious tone, 'if you're going to talk business—and I suppose that's the reason he's coming here—I'll get out of your way.'

'Business!' Ewan's laugh was harsh. 'Well, yes, I guess that's what it is ... No, wait, Roz.' He turned away from the window and his contemplation of the cold April sunset and went over to the wide fireplace. For a moment he stared sombrely at the blaze, nudging a log into place with his foot, and sending up a stream of sparks. 'Hold on a minute. There's something I must tell you.'

Arrested by his tone, Roz put down the tray, her dark, clear eyebrows raised questioningly. The firelight washed over Ewan's thin face, and despite the bombshell he had dropped Roz felt her heart move with pity for him. In eight months he had aged. It was as if the death of his fiancée on that Welsh mountainside last August had destroyed all his youth.

'Well, go on,' she prompted gently. 'What is it?'

He moved the log again. 'Hard to know where to begin,' he jerked out. 'Since Lisa died I've ... Oh, hell, Roz, no sense in beating about the bush.' He turned anguished eyes towards her. 'I've landed myself in one hell of a mess. And that,' he went on bitterly, 'is an understatement. No, don't interrupt. Just listen. This isn't easy. ...' Then his words came in a spate, pouring out as if he wanted to spill the story quickly and get it over with. 'I started gambling. Not much, at first. But it grew. It became a—a fever, I suppose. A compulsion.' His bark of laughter sent a shiver through Roz. 'Oh, I can't explain it, much less justify it. And I don't suppose anyone would understand this, but at the time it was a way of—well, of looking forward ... Kind of projecting myself into a future. The past was painful, the present was hell ... without Lisa. In some crazy way it seemed to help me to deal with—just *time*, I guess.'

'I think I can see that,' Roz murmured softly. 'I'm sure no one would blame you for——'

Ewan held up an admonitory hand. 'Wait till you hear
the rest. Not that it's in any way original.' Again, the
chilling laugh. 'I got into debt. Heavily. And then—then
I bought a half-share in a racehorse with Paul Martel;
he put up the money.'

Roz's eyes widened, but Ewan went on, tapping out
the words in a relentless staccato rhythm. 'It had po-
tential, you see. At least, that's what I understood. It
could have cleared my debts. A couple of good races...
That's the way I saw it.' He shrugged, a gesture of defeat.
'Instead it went lame. It'll never be much good now.'

He stopped, and for a moment the only sound was
the crackle of flames in the grate. Then Roz said tentatively, 'How much do you owe, Ewan?'

His eyes seemed unfocused in his strained face. 'I
daren't tell you that, Roz. I wish I didn't have to tell
you any of it. But I'm in debt to Paul Martel and——'

'I think I see,' Roz said thoughtfully. 'That's the
reason why Nick's coming over tonight? Is that it?'
Anger cracked a sudden whiplash in her normally low
voice. 'Big brother Nick is coming to put the pressure
on?'

Ewan dragged up a deep sigh and raked his hand
though his fair hair. 'Something like that, I guess.'

'Is there anything I can do?' Roz was thinking fran-
tically, her mind still trying to recover from the twin
blows. She never wanted to come face to face with Nick
Martel again; she had put him out of her life two years
ago after an endless night of soul-searching. But at this
moment even his visit here seemed trivial compared with
Ewan's problems. Racehorses cost a great deal of money;
then there was stabling and feed bills, veterinary fees,
trainers, tack... Oh, the list was endless. Ewan must
have been out of his mind! What did he know about
horses, anyway? Certainly less than Paul Martel. 'What

can I say?' she whispered. 'But you know I'll help if I can. I could raise a little money, I think.'

Ewan smiled suddenly, his mouth young and sweet for a moment. 'Thanks, Rozzie, but no.'

'But there has got to be *some* way out... The bank, perhaps?' she urged.

'I'm already overdrawn and getting letters from the manager. No, I'll just have to eat humble pie and ask for time to pay. But it's going to take a lifetime.' Then he straightened up, as if bracing himself. 'But listen,' he went on firmly, 'the only reason I've burdened you with all this is to explain why Nick's coming over. And I would prefer it if you made yourself scarce for an hour or so. It's not going to be at all pleasant.' He smiled again rue-fully. 'Sorry,' he murmured. 'You've always been the sensible one, my strong little sister, the bearer of burdens. But this isn't your problem. I'll try and sort something out. One thing I've learned: I'll never gamble again, and that's got to be good news, hasn't it?'

Roz sensed that he was trying to reassure her, and she forced an answering grin. 'Yes, I'm sure you're right— I mean about sorting something out.' She picked up the tray again. 'Well, I'll wash these cups and then get back to my workshop.' She turned in the doorway. 'Ewan,' she began diffidently, 'don't eat too big a portion of humble pie. Martels might have lived at Meronthorpe since time out of mind, and Nick might be a high-flyer, but he's not God. So don't let him treat you as if he were. Promise?'

'I'll bear it in mind. And—Roz? Thanks for not...well, for being so—decent about things.'

Roz carried the tray through the dining-room. One table-lamp burnished the old oak panelling in a soft sheen that never failed to please her eye, but tonight she was blind to it. Too many other things on her mind jostled for attention. Absently she washed the crockery and put it away. Then she shrugged into the old duffel coat which she and Ewan shared indiscriminately for outside jobs, and made her way across the cobbled courtyard to the old stable which had been adapted as a workshop.

If the worse came to the worst, she decided numbly, Grey Garth could be sold. So Ewan's problems weren't absolutely insoluble. They could find somewhere else— a small flat or bungalow away from the dale, where property tended to be expensive; they could move nearer to York, where Ewan's office was. But to sell Grey Garth now... She winced at the prospect.

The house had been left jointly to her and Ewan in their mother's will six years ago. Too big, too old, too expensive to run, it would have been sensible to sell it then. But, broken up by their mother's death, neither she nor Ewan could face the thought of leaving it. Then, during a freak storm the following March, part of the roof had been torn off, revealing other damage. Grey Garth had to be re-roofed and the structural faults made good. And to pay for it they had sold off the west side of the house.

It had worked out well, for Anna and Piet Sloot, a prosperous Dutch couple house-hunting in the Yorkshire Dales, had immediately fallen in love with Grey Garth. And as they spent only four months of the year in England they were happy that Roz and Ewan were on the spot to keep an eye on things. From Roz's point of view there was no denying that the smaller living quarters made life easier and cheaper, while enabling her and Ewan to stay on in the place that meant home.

She switched on the light in the workshop and drew the thick curtains against the darkness outside, wishing that she could shut out thoughts of Nick as easily. Of all the people Ewan could have chosen as partner in his hare-brained scheme, why, oh, why had it had to be Nick's younger brother Paul?

Determinedly she thrust aside the speculations which crowded her mind. There was nothing she could do until Nick had been and gone. She turned on the radio, switched on the coffee machine and picked up the battered doll she was restoring. Its face stared blankly up at her and, as always, she was gripped by the magic of its history, wondering how many childish hands had nursed it during the past hundred years or so.

As with many wax-faced dolls, its nose had been damaged. Carefully she warmed the wax cheeks with a piece of heated flannel until they softened slightly, then, working with infinite care and patience, she smoothed the wax towards the centre, building up the tip of the nose. It was a slow and painstaking task, absorbing her totally, and progressing almost imperceptibly towards an acceptable result. She needed the distraction for, apart from Ewan's disastrous news, the knowledge that Nick was actually coming here to Grey Garth had revived emotions which she had told herself were long since dead.

At last she put the doll down. Some hair needed replacing, and the cotton body casing had split, leaking bran. Roz's shoulders ached, and she glanced at her watch. Almost nine. She stood up, stretching. Pushing back the dark, straight bob which swung just above her shoulders, she had a sudden blinding mental picture of Nick.

Nick. Probably at this very moment his head was hollowing the cushion of her chair by the fire as he sat facing Ewan. Memory painted his image with stunning clarity; she could visualise those hazel-gold eyes narrowing coldly as he stripped Ewan of any pride he had left. She blinked quickly, trying to kill the image, but one picture unrolled into another, and she caught herself wondering painfully how the past two years might have changed Nick.

But why should he have changed at all? Except in that he had two more years of experience to add to the other thirty-four. Two years of—what? Of making money, building up the Martel holiday empire; two years of playing the lover; two years of deception, lies, womanising . . . Even their very first meeting had shown her . . .

It had been at Ilona Ransome's party. Roz was nursing a glass of white wine and complimenting Ilona on her Christmas decorations when suddenly she had looked up to see a man shouldering his way through the guests. He had the kind of confidence of bearing that needed to make no statements. Thick hair, the warm brown of beech leaves in autumn, cheekbones and jawline catching the light in hard, polished gleams, a formal dark grey suit worn with the panache of a man who, knowing the excellence of cloth and cut, wore it as a second skin. As he approached, an uneven curl of a sensuously moulded mouth quickened her blood. It had all happened in a second. The room came into focus again. Roz heard the music, the background hum of several conversations, and her own voice saying, 'Ewan was so sorry he had to miss this, Ilona, but he had to go to——'

Then the stranger was beside them, the smile still there, the eyes capturing Roz's gaze for a second before, unpredictably, she looked away in confusion. Then he said quietly, 'Ilona, I'd like you to introduce me, please. Something tells me that this is one occasion when things should be done correctly.'

'Dominic Martel, Roz Parrish,' Ilona laughed. 'So glad you managed to come, Nick. Sam's wanting a word with you.'

'And I'm very glad you invited me.' But Nick was looking into Roz's face as he took her hand, and she saw the golden flecks dance in the clear hazel eyes.

'Well, I'll leave you two to get acquainted,' Ilona murmured. 'Where *is* Sam? Really, some husbands...' She moved away.

'Where shall we start?' Nick said. 'Perhaps by dancing?' As if Roz's silence was consent, he took her glass from her and set it down. Then, as his hands drew her towards him, 'And we could progress a little if you told me what Roz is short for. Rosalind?'

Roz had a penetrating conviction that things were happening too fast and too smoothly. The ease with which his tall frame accommodated hers, moving in rhythmic unison, strengthened her reservations. He was just too attractive, she thought, and too sure of his effect.

She leaned slightly away from him. 'No. Rosamund,' she said briefly. 'But everyone calls me Roz.'

'Then *I* shall call you Rosamund—*rosa mundi*—rose of the world. It suits you.' His voice was low and sleepy, and against all reason Roz was suddenly suffused by a strange weakness which she tried, cynically, to dismiss.

But, in spite of all logic, her initial resistance waned as he talked, persuasively drawing from her a softening response which soon eased them into an animated exchange of views, discovering that they had the same tastes in music, food, humour, art. He was holding her more closely, his left hand cradling her right hand against his chest almost protectively.

'So you restore old dolls, dolls' houses, small furniture,' he murmured afterwards when they were sitting together on a sofa in the corner of the softly lit room. He took her hands, turning them over and scrutinising them, then said, 'Yes, there is delicacy, sensitivity, yet strength...'

Slowly she withdrew them, fighting down a sudden breathlessness, determined to hold on to her common sense which told her that this man was altogether too practised, too skilful. And that she, Roz Parrish—practical and, at times, slightly aloof—should be falling for these hammed-up gambits was beyond all comprehension. Then his eyes trapped her gaze again, and she knew it wasn't.

'And what do you do?' she asked brightly.

'My work is other people's leisure.' He went on to speak of holiday developments, leisure parks, educational projects, and the places where his work took him. Totally absorbed, she didn't see Sam Ransome approach until he was standing before them.

'Hate to interrupt you two,' he said, 'but could you spare me a few minutes some time, Nick? I need your advice. Ilona and I are thinking of acquiring a holiday home on the Algarve. I've got the details in my study, and I'd like you to vet a couple of points.' He looked past Nick to Roz. 'Sorry, but I won't keep him long.'

Nick stood up. 'Excuse me, Rosamund. Seems I must sing for my supper. Don't go away.'

Bemused, Roz watched Nick follow Sam out of the room, then she stood up. It was warm in here, and she needed to get herself together again. Slowly she went upstairs and through the guest-room with its twin beds laden with guests' coats. In the adjoining bathroom she half closed the door behind her. She hardly recognised her reflection; her eyes held a starriness that eclipsed their usual thoughtful light. Even her mouth—the feature which she so often deplored because of its width—curved softly. She ran her fingers through her hair, lifting the curly, negligent tumble away from her warm neck, and watched it settle back into a style which she hadn't been too sure about until this minute.

Then, dimly at first, she became aware of voices in the bedroom.

'I should have got here earlier,' a rather high voice complained, 'before he started making a play for that dark girl. Roz something-or-other. I think they've both slipped away, so he remains true to form—good old Nick!'

There was a low murmur, then the high voice resumed, 'Only a couple of months ago he seemed besotted with Melody Hargreaves. I suppose if she hadn't gone off on that cruise the affair would still be going on. Melody came back today, I believe, but obviously our Nick didn't intend to mark time until she's able to pick up the threads again.'

There came an amused laugh and a voice said, 'Thank heaven I'm married and out of it all.'

'So is Melody. Married, I mean. But she's very much *in* it all. By the way, I'm giving a party in the New Year. I think I'll invite Nick. I could tell him that Melody will be there. Then, on the night, I'll say she had to cancel.'

The low laugh came again. 'And so leave the field clear for you. Sarah Armitage, just what depths will you sink to? All this scheming just so that you can get your hot little hands on Nick. Or is it his money?'

'I don't know. Why separate the two? Either way, it's an attractively packaged deal.' The voices faded, and Roz realised that they had left the bedroom.

So her first instincts had been right. Nick—'running true to form.' And Melody—a married woman. I might have guessed, Roz thought. Well, I *did* guess, instinctively. She grimaced at her reflection. She didn't really want to go back to the party. She glanced at her watch. She was going to an auction the following day and needed to make an early start so that she would have plenty of time to view before the sale began.

She snapped her handbag shut, collected her coat and went down. Sarah Armitage—whoever she was—had a clear field now. Feel free, Roz thought, with a wry twist of her mouth. Nick Martel's all yours. And anyone else's, by the look of things.

She let herself out of the house. In the morning she would phone Ilona and Sam, make her excuses and thank them.

Three days later she was returning home after an errand. Ewan's car had gone to be serviced, and he had borrowed hers, so she had taken out her old bicycle and was enjoying the exercise and the landscape as it lay waiting for snow, when an ominous rattle from the back wheel warned of a puncture.

It could be worse. She was only a mile away from Hexby, a mile and a half from Grey Garth. She would be home before dark. Already the first flakes of snow were dappling the road ahead, sitting on her eyelashes for a moment before melting. She turned up the collar of her sheepskin and trudged on.

A Range Rover overtook her and stopped just ahead, then the door opened, and a voice which had been running through her brain for the last three days said, 'Trouble?'

A wave of heat flowed up into her face. 'Oh . . . hello. Just a puncture. I'll soon be home,' she mumbled.

The golden eyes narrowed between thick lashes as he watched her for a moment. 'You're an independent lady, aren't you?' Almost before she realised his intention he had swung open the tailgate and lifted the bicycle into the back of the Range Rover. 'Get in. I'll take you home.'

'And you're a masterful gentleman, aren't you,' she retorted lamely. She was alarmed by the tingle that shimmered inside her.

'Don't tell me you would prefer to walk—in this?' The snow was thickening, whirling and eddying, mingling whitening earth with swollen yellow-grey sky.

'No, of course not. Thank you.' She got into the car and he closed the door and went round to the driver's side.

'I have to make a call on the way, but it shouldn't take more than ten minutes, all right?' He glanced sideways at her, but she fastened her gaze on the golden lights that streamed ahead as she nodded. 'You slipped away from the party,' he said after a moment, in a matter-of-fact voice.

'I didn't want a late night,' she explained coolly. Her heartbeat seemed to have strengthened, and it appeared that their earlier intimacy was in danger of redeveloping. She couldn't help but be aware of his body, of the brown hands on the wheel, the amber moleskin-covered thighs, the breadth of his shoulders beneath the mingled tawny and amber wool of his thick sweater.

'You might at least have said goodnight,' he returned idly.

'I thought you were busy with Sam.' In spite of the desultory tone of their conversation, the atmosphere seemed to prickle with tension, and she was relieved when he drew up before a small cottage. 'My old nanny,' he explained. 'I always take her a few Christmas goodies. Coming in with me?'

'I don't think so,' she said.

'Oh, for heaven's sake! What's the matter? Are you planning to slip away again?'

'Of course not,' she said stiffly. 'It's just——'

'You know, you can be very trying at times, Rosamund.' His use of her name warmed something inside her. 'Let's not stay here arguing. Come along. I think I can promise you a glass of elderberry wine. You'll be quite safe, you know,' he added, his eyes narrowing.

'I didn't suspect otherwise,' she said loftily. 'I can take care of myself.' She watched him lift a large carton from the back and followed him to the door of the cottage, determined to keep her distance despite the insidious and utterly unreasonable happiness she felt at seeing him again. And that in itself should have been a warning.

His height dominated the tiny room, and he had to stoop to avoid the overhead beams. 'A little Christmas cheer,' he said, bending to kiss the rosy, wrinkled face with its pursed mouth held up to his. He put the box on the table. 'And something for your arthritis, too. And I've brought a friend—Miss Parrish.'

Faded blue eyes shone as the old woman took Roz's hand. 'You're a good boy, Dominic,' she murmured. 'You never forget me.'

'How could I,' he quipped, 'when you're the only woman who ever managed to keep me in order?'

'Aye, and it took a deal of doing. A lively young sprig you were.' She turned to Roz. 'He thought he could run circles around me. I remember——'

'Oh, no,' Nick groaned, 'not another of your stories! What are you doing on Christmas Day?'

'Same as any other day, I expect.'

The old woman reached into a corner cupboard and brought down three glasses. None of them matched, but each was delicately etched, and when Roz admired them Nick said, 'Rosamund appreciates antiques.'

'Oh? Then what's she doing with you?' came the sharp retort. Then, laughing at her own wit, Miss Berridge poured them each a glass of wine and sat down.

'I'll send a car over for you on Christmas Day,' Nick resumed. 'You'll eat Christmas dinner with us.'

'Only if you promise to behave. None of your jokes. And you can tell Paul that, too.'

Roz glanced at Nick and caught his eye. He gave the ghost of a wink. This didn't seem the same man as the one who was being discussed in Ilona's guest-room, and Roz felt herself drawn to him again. It was difficult not to laugh at Miss Berridge's acid observations which obviously clothed a deep affection for Nick.

'That's settled, then,' Nick said at last, getting up. 'We'll pick you up about eleven-thirty.'

'Will you be there too, Miss Parrish?' The old woman reached for her stick and took Roz's arm to help herself to her feet.

'Not so fast, Nanny,' Nick said quickly. 'I'm still working on it.'

The world outside was white and still, and the snow creaked beneath their feet as they went back to the car.

'She's nice,' Roz said as she turned to wave towards the window where Miss Berridge was standing, watching. 'I wish you hadn't put a stop to her tale-telling, though.' She laughed roguishly.

Nick gave her a long, level look. 'It's the me of today who I hope would interest you more,' he said quietly. 'And what about Christmas Day? Am I going to have to work hard at it, or will you simply say "yes" here and now and avoid a tedious argument?'

Roz turned to look at him. Their eyes met and held. The white stillness around seemed to encroach, wrapping them in hushed enchantment. 'Yes,' she whispered. He leaned towards her, and she saw his mouth for a second before it was laid on hers. She caught her breath raggedly, pulling back and turning her head violently to stare out of the window, her heart racing.

That evening, over coffee, she asked Ewan what he would be doing on Christmas Day.

'Well, I thought we would be spending it here, as usual,' he said. 'Why?'

'I've been invited to Meronthorpe. I met Nick Martel at Ilona's party.'

Ewan gave a low whistle, frowning. 'Be careful, Rozzie. That guy's reputation isn't exactly unblemished.'

'Idle gossip,' Roz retorted, surprised to hear the defensive note in her voice. 'And silly women who throw themselves at him.'

'Well, I suppose he is quite a catch. All the same, I wouldn't like you to——'

'Don't worry about me, Ewan.' Roz's tone softened. 'I'm twenty-three, remember? I'm a big girl and can look after myself.'

'OK, then I'll spend the day with Lisa. You haven't met her yet, but you'll like her.'

It was a real country-house Christmas. Blazing fires, hot rum punch for visitors who came and went, the church choir standing on the priceless Persian carpet in the hall singing "Christians Awake", Nanny Berridge in a high-backed chair by the fire, her shoulders draped in a lilac-coloured shawl—an extra present from Paul and Nick. And Nick's father, ramrod straight, brusquely spoken but suddenly unbending and taking Roz away to see his collection of armorial porcelain, some of which had been made for the Empress Eugenie. And, of course, Nick... Laughter, warmth, tortoiseshell eyes, mistletoe kisses...

It set the tone for the spring that followed. Roz ignored the subtle hints she encountered, the occasional obvious jealousy. She knew Nick better than anyone else, didn't she?

The coffee machine gave a sudden loud hiss, snapping her back to the present. She went to the door, biting her lip, trying to quell the memories that still clamoured. Surely Nick would have left by now. But supposing he hadn't? Restlessly she went back to the shabby old sofa and flopped down; she wasn't going to risk a meeting with him.

They had been right, she thought, those people who had warned her against Nick. So when the end came she couldn't even plead ignorance. She had simply fallen into the age-old trap of believing that, with *her*, Nick was different. A happy fool in a fool's paradise, until the evening of her twenty-fourth birthday, when she was forced to accept the truth that leopards didn't change their spots.

She couldn't even bear to see him again after that rainy evening. And in a telephone call to him at Meronthorpe the following morning only her pride prevented her telling him how she had seen him, and the girl with him, when he was supposed to have been in Birmingham. Later that morning Roz had driven to Chester, heartbreak and despair demanding that she get right away from the area. And Sally, good old schoolfriend Sally, had been delighted by the visit and had insisted that Roz stay.

Two days later a letter had arrived at Chester; presumably Nick had asked Ewan for Roz's address. Roz thrust it into the kitchen boiler as soon as she recognised the handwriting on the envelope. Nothing, but nothing, that Nick might say could change things.

Two weeks later when she returned to Hexby she learned with a mixture of agony and relief that Nick had gone abroad and would be away for some time.

With a little start she came back to the present again. It was stupid not to have guessed that, inevitably, their paths would cross again, but never in a million years could she have predicted the dire circumstances which would bring him into her home.

Giving herself a mental shake, she started sorting through a basket of scraps of old material, setting aside those which would be suitable for dressing the wax-faced doll. The eyes of other dolls in varying stages of dilapidation seemed to watch her. Again she wondered if Nick had left yet; she couldn't bear the suspense much longer. Time seemed frozen.

She was at the far end of the workshop, riffling through an encyclopedia of period costume, when the door opened.

'Oh, Ewan...' she began, swinging round, tension tautening her features. Then she stopped, petrified by the sight of Nick standing there. Her stomach seemed to fill with ice-water as her heart began to lurch sick-eningly. Her hand groped for support and found the bookshelf. She leaned against it gratefully. At last she managed to say in a wintry voice, 'Don't you ever knock?'

'I did. Don't you ever listen?' His eyes were slitted to a mere gleam between the bristly lashes, and there was a quality of enormous stillness in his stance. He brought in with him the smell of clean, cold air underlain with a woody, masculine fragrance which seemed to blow the past right back into her face.

CHAPTER TWO

HE hadn't changed much, she thought dully through her shock. His hair still had that beech-leaf tint, his skin held the golden warmth of foreign suns. In the summer, she knew, he would go very dark. She used to call him her 'brown man' in those other days... Her breath caught for a moment. But had he always been quite so—so *commanding*? And his smile so disarmingly attractive? Yes, yes, yes, an inner voice half sobbed. It was his ammunition, to be trained on any woman who, for a variety of reasons, might interest him temporarily. As she had once done. Was it that, after the sophisticated beauties of his circle, he had found her refreshingly different? *Quaint?* Until his needs dictated something more exotic?

Somehow, among past memories and present impressions, she found her voice again, and it was satisfyingly cool. 'What is it you want? I thought your business was with Ewan.'

'It was. That's all been taken care of now, but I wasn't going to pass up the chance of dropping in on an old friend. That would have been impolite under the circumstances, don't you think? And we were friends—once. Weren't we, Rosamund?'

She turned away, sliding the book into its place on the shelf with hands that fumbled. Nick was still the only person ever to use her full given name, allowing his husky, vibrant voice to slide over each syllable like a caress. During the past two years she had made herself forget that, along with so many other things. And she didn't need him here now to refresh her memory!

'Yes,' she said blandly, 'we *were* friends once. But it's a long time ago. Who was it who said, "Gathered flowers are dead"?' She tilted her head back, widening her mouth in an impartial smile. 'And I expect you've gathered an awful lot of *friends* since then.'

Lights danced in his eyes. 'Well, I wouldn't want to boast, of course,' he murmured. 'But don't they also say that old friends are the best friends?' He glanced around at the shelf of dolls, and at the stencilled and painted pine furniture which was Roz's latest venture, wrinkling his nose at the smells of turpentine and linseed oil, beeswax, paint. 'I do believe I detect the aroma of success,' he said lightly. 'It looks as if you're very busy.'

'Oh, I am,' she said carelessly, then looked at him sharply. Was he now going to lead the conversation into financial channels?

But he didn't speak. Instead he watched her, with a half-smile printing an attractive fan of lines at the corners of his eyes. She felt a warm wave creep upwards from her toes to the crown of her head, melting the inner ice. She seemed unable to drag her eyes away from his face. And, as if he recognised his power, his smile widened as, with an easy, relaxed movement, he dropped down on the battered sofa. 'Well,' he prompted gently, 'aren't you going to offer me a coffee? Your brother's hospitality didn't extend so far.'

Naturally it didn't, Roz thought sharply, suddenly recalling the reason behind Nick's visit. Ewan had more important things on his mind. She ached to learn the outcome of their talk, but had no intention of asking Nick. It was up to Ewan to tell her as much as he wanted her to know.

'I was sorry to hear of your father's illness,' she said at last, handing him a mug.

He took it, staring down at the dark liquid. 'You remember how I like it,' he remarked. 'Black and strong with half a spoon of sugar. What a memory. I wonder what else you remember?' His tone seemed to have slipped a key lower into slumbrous, suggestive depths of intimacy. To Roz's intense irritation she felt the stirrings of an old excitement and sternly quelled them.

'I remember that I always got along very well with your father,' she said crisply.

Nick's laugh was a white flash in his tan. 'All right, I take your point.' His voice changed, became flatter and matter of fact. 'The old man has a high regard for you, too. Why don't you go over and see him? It would cheer him.'

Roz shot him a cynical glance. 'Perhaps I will,' she said, then added very softly, 'When will you be going away again?'

Nick's laugh echoed through the stable. 'You really love spelling it out, don't you, Rosamund?'

'Only if I must,' she answered smoothly. 'And now I suppose that as this unexpected visit has assumed all the trappings of a conventional social call, perhaps I ought to ask what you've been doing these past two years.'

Nick eyed her with cool amusement, his gaze sliding over the smooth dark hair, the long, slightly obliquely set dark eyes, to rest on the full, wide mouth before dropping to the open-necked shirt she wore belted over tight red trousers. Then he leaned back, completely at ease, one arm resting along the back of the sofa. Roz was uncomfortably aware of his nearness. 'This and that,' he said laconically. 'Travelling a lot, looking at sites, getting in on the ground floor of holiday developments. Why? Are you looking for a glamorous job?'

'Certainly not,' she retorted. 'I've got a job which pleases me more than anything you could offer.' She wished that he would hurry and drink his coffee and leave her in peace. Only one thing was important to-night, and that was Ewan's plans and the outcome of his talk with Nick. And Nick must sense her eagerness to get back to the house. But apparently it amused him to keep her pinned down here in a typical display of male domination.

She glanced pointedly at her watch, then looked up sharply as he said, 'Good—because I wondered how you would feel about giving it up.'

She thought that the remark held a veiled threat. Could it be an oblique hint that she might have to leave Grey Garth because of Ewan's money troubles? She stared at him, trying to read his meaning.

His eyes met hers, holding them. Still watching her, he put down his mug and then, slowly, reached for her hand. For one dreamlike moment she let herself be drawn closer to him. How easy it would be, and how wonderful, to lie with her head on his shoulder and feel his strength close around her in a cocoon which offered escape from her worries, comfort and the reassurance that she wasn't alone... But this was Nick Martel, she reminded herself tartly, the last person to be relied upon or to trust.

She pulled away from him, brushing off his hand. 'Look,' she said, avoiding his eyes, 'you and I have nothing to say to each other. And if your business with Ewan is done then there's absolutely no reason for you to stay. You didn't come to see *me*, to pay me the com-pliment of looking up an old friend!'

Abruptly she got up and went towards the door. She was beyond caring about politeness. Why should she bother? He had made a fool of her once. How many lies had he told her during those months which she had thought idyllic? So who the hell did he think he was to come back and parade his charm before her once again? She lifted her hand to the latch, but he didn't get up.

Instead he slewed round, looking at her over the back of the sofa, the severe symmetry of his features hardening suddenly.

'You're wrong, Rosamund,' he told her coolly. 'In a sense, my business with Ewan also concerns you. So perhaps you had better come back here and listen—that is, if you're at all interested in keeping your brother out of trouble.'

'Of course I'm interested,' she snapped. 'But don't worry, he'll pay your brother every penny he owes.'

'Really?' Nick's eyebrows rose in cynical amusement. 'What with, I wonder? Ewan hasn't any money. He's spent it. Lost it. Heavens, Rosamund, don't you know the extent of his stupidity? I thought you two were pretty close. And couldn't you have stopped him before he went so far?'

'I would have,' she flashed, 'if I had known. But he only told me about it this evening.' Wearily she pushed back her hair. 'I'm not excusing him, but . . . Well, I can sympathise.' Unthinkingly, she sank down again beside Nick. 'Lisa—Ewan's fiancée—died. They were to go climbing with another couple one weekend, then Ewan had to cry off because of an overseas visitor coming on business. So, rather than have Lisa cancel her weekend, he persuaded her to go with the others.' Roz hesitated, then went on more quietly, 'Ewan blamed himself. He said that if he hadn't insisted, or if he had been there instead of chasing work, the accident wouldn't have happened.'

Her voice died as she remembered those bleak, terrible days, Ewan's remorse and self-accusation, the grief that had turned him into a robot, functioning as programmed, but without thought or heart. The room was silent except for a faint, erratic hiss from the coffee machine. Then she went on tonelessly, 'Is it too difficult for you to—understand? He tried to find some kind of—

solace... He made—mistakes.' She faced Nick again, her eyes hard. 'But obviously the human aspects aren't your concern. You're simply thinking of——'

'For heaven's sake, be quiet and listen to me for a minute,' Nick rasped, turning suddenly and taking both her hands in a crushing grip. 'I'm trying to explain why I've come to see *you*. I'm not here to praise or condemn.'

'No, you're here to get your pound of flesh. Or should I say your brother's pound of flesh? To hell with the cause of Ewan's troubles. What does his heartbreak matter, after all? *This* is business; the Martels must get their money. Well, I've told you,' she blazed, 'you'll get it. Every last penny. One way or another we'll——'

'Shut *up*!' Nick roared. 'And just listen. Have you any idea just how much he owes? And not only to Paul. There are other creditors too, you know. Well, have you?'

Roz shook her head. 'No, Ewan wouldn't tell me.'

'Then if he wouldn't, I certainly won't.'

Roz wrenched her hands away. 'Well, whatever the amount, we'll find it somehow. We—we'll sell Grey Garth if we must. Isn't that what you were hinting at earlier?'

Nick sat back, a flicker of grim amusement twisting the sensuous line of his mouth, but his voice was deceptively gentle as he pointed out, 'You've already sold the biggest part of it—to the Sloots.'

'Then we'll just have to sell the rest,' said Roz staunchly.

For a moment Nick stared at her, his eyes thoughtful. Then he said quietly, 'Poor Rosamund, you really have no idea of the size of your brother's problems, have you? I'm sorry, my dear, but your home wouldn't raise enough to clear his debts.'

'I don't believe you,' she whispered. 'And don't "poor Rosamund" me! I don't need your pity. Anyway, I think you're lying. You're trying to frighten me. There's got to be a mistake.'

'There have been several,' said Nick drily. 'And the biggest was a racehorse called Akhbar. Didn't he even tell you about that?'

Roz was silent. Her heart seemed to have plunged into a dark, frightening abyss. She couldn't think. She had supposed that, at worst, Ewan might owe a few thousand; bad enough, but not beyond clearing in time if they both worked hard. But obviously she had underestimated the sum. Her eyes searched Nick's, hoping to read a lie there but finding only a steadfast hazel-gold gaze.

She looked away, dropping her head into her hands and closing her eyes against the pressure of misery. She felt Nick's arm go around her shoulder, and she tensed, lifting her head. 'Obviously I didn't know the half of it,' she whispered. 'As I told you, I hadn't an inkling until this evening, and it's all—rather a lot to—to take in... What are we to do? You must know how these things work.' Her voice failed, but she forced herself on. 'So we're—ruined. Ruined! What an outdated expression that is.' Her laugh hovered on an unsteady note, but she controlled it quickly. 'Is there—any way out?'

For a moment Nick didn't speak. Even the coffee-maker had stopped its faint noise, and the workshop held a silence as thick and oppressive as a forest. Then he said in an expressionless voice, 'There just *might* be something. It depends on you, Rosamund. That's why I came to see you.'

Roz sat up quickly, a glimmer of hope illuminating her pale face. 'I'll do anything,' she said fervently. 'Anything to help.'

'Steady, my dear,' said Nick calmly. 'Don't go over the top. You might not welcome my suggestion, so let's not be rash until you've heard it.'

'But I *meant* it,' Roz insisted. '*Anything* I can do...'

'Well, there is one thing.' Nick's tone was laconic, so that, when he spoke again, for one shattering moment Roz was sure she hadn't heard him correctly. 'You can marry me, Rosamund.'

She stared at him for what seemed an eternity, frozen in some hideous limbo. His face told her nothing. Only his mouth moved in a slightly mocking smile that didn't reach his eyes.

'What—what did you say?' she stammered at last.

'I think you heard well enough. I asked you to marry me. Perhaps you would prefer me to spell it out? Or put it in writing?'

She scowled at him. 'You're being utterly ridiculous! And cruel, too!' She jumped up and stood over him, her eyes dancing with angry tears. 'If this is your idea of a joke, then I don't applaud your timing. You had better go!' She shook her head from side to side. 'Oh, Nick, I learned some things about you two years ago, but I never suspected you of such sick, twisted humour.' She was trembling. Two years ago she would have given her all to hear him ask just such a question. She had almost anticipated it, sensing that their relationship was leading to a proposal of marriage. She had imagined it happening while she was in his arms, or on one of those Sunday afternoons they spent together. Winter, by the great fire at Meronthorpe, toasting muffins and listening to Mahler or Beethoven as the twilight deepened. Or in the intimacy of their special alcove in their favourite restaurant. Not that she had needed the trimmings, but they would have been there anyway—as they always were, with Nick—to enhance every moment they spent together. And now—*this*!

'You—you had just better go,' she said, hardly able to speak. 'Get out. Just go. You and your brother between you have certainly——'

'Well,' Nick interrupted with a calm reason that fired her anger higher, 'I *did* warn you that you might not like my idea. But hold on a moment, Rosamund. Let's hear *your* suggestion for getting out of this mess of your brother's making.'

'I've had no time to think yet,' she sparked. 'But I'll come up with something. Don't worry. There's got to be *some* way out of——'

Nick stood up. 'There is. I've just told you. Well, I admire your spirit, my dear. You're not going to find it easy, though. Of course, Ewan could always pack his bags and flee the country.'

'How *dare* you be so flippant?' she breathed. 'Can't you see that ... Oh, to think that once I——'

'I'm not being flippant. He wouldn't be the first person to skip off in this kind of situation. And that would leave you alone, with a scandal on your hands. Just think of the vicarious pleasure you would give to some of the old biddies in the village! You wouldn't enjoy it one bit! So why not think over my proposition? Or should I say proposal? It sounds better.' When she didn't answer, but just stood glaring at him, he murmured, 'It's a way out for you, and I think I can safely promise you a very comfortable life-style. And,' he went on in velvet tones, 'you needn't worry that I would make any unwelcome demands upon you. Separate rooms ... I imagine that would be one of your conditions if, in fact, you do decide to consider it.'

'You read me like a book,' she said scathingly.

'And,' he continued, as if she hadn't spoken, 'I wouldn't interfere too much in your life, and I would expect the same consideration from you. After all, I'm away much of the time, so that should simplify the whole thing.'

She stared up at him. The whole evening, and he himself, seemed unreal, without credibility. Only the smells of the workshop and the blank gaze of the dolls were real. 'You had it all prepared when you walked in here, didn't you?' she breathed. 'But I can't believe that even you are conceited enough to think that I would seriously consider such a crazy scheme for even one moment.' She paused, then went on shrewdly, 'But one thing does arouse my curiosity. What would be in it for you, Nick? I'm not so utterly naïve as to think you're making this offer out of the kindness of your heart. And if your—conditions are as they say, then why marry at all? Why bother? So tell me, just what do *you* expect to gain from such a deal?'

'Me?' He swung his car keys thoughtfully. 'Well, let me put it this way. A married man carries an aura of stability, purpose, a stake in the future. Even in this day and age marriage is part of the traditional, established pattern, the ideal state. Also you would fill a gap as a very decorative and useful appendage. Your company at various business conferences and social functions would—shall we say consolidate?—my image.'

'How very neat. And that's all?' she said coldly.

'Not quite,' His mouth tightened into a hard line. The golden glints were gone from his eyes, there was just amber ice, and she shivered. 'No, not quite all. You made a fool of me once, Rosamund,' he said softly. 'You played me along to the stage where I...' Then his tone crisped. 'And then you dropped me with one single telephone call. "I'm not into heavy relationships," you said. As if that explained everything.'

'I see. You mean I beat you at your own game, and you didn't like it.'

He stared at her coldly. 'I wasn't aware at the time that it *was* a game.'

'Do you really expect me to believe that?' She gave a mirthless laugh. 'So this—this pitiful proposal is my come-uppance?' Against all her intentions, Roz began

to laugh, a high note that jarred in her own ears and
went on and on. It had nothing to do with amusement,
and she seemed incapable of stopping it.

Nick came back from the door and gripped her
shoulders, shaking her sharply. 'Stop it,' he ordered. 'Do
you hear? Rosamund, that's *enough*.'

His note of authority braced her against the hysteria
which threatened to overwhelm her, and she felt herself
steadying. 'Does—does Ewan know of this—solution of
yours?' she whispered when she judged it safe to speak
again.

'Of course not. I've left the idiot to stew in his own
juice. Let him worry a while longer. It'll do him good.'

'It's like a nightmare,' she said dully. 'Only this
morning, everything was quite different. Somehow I
can't quite grasp it all. Unreal. It's all so grotesquely
unreal.'

'Give it time,' Nick said. 'Whichever way you choose,
you'll find it's reality all right.'

'Choose?' she echoed. 'You don't seriously expect me
to take the way out that you've offered, do you? Anyway,
Ewan would be—devastated if he knew that I was repaying his debts by marrying *you*.'

'Really?' Nick drawled. 'I wouldn't take a bet on that.
Oh, I do beg your pardon, bet is a dirty word at the
moment, isn't it?' As she glared at him, he went on, 'All
right, I apologise. He is your brother, so perhaps I
shouldn't have said that. But he's weak, Rosamund.
Weak enough to allow another damn fool like my own
brother to persuade him into this half-baked scheme of
investing in a racehorse, for pete's sake! What does either
of them know about the turf, anyway? Racehorses are
a rich man's hobby, not an income supplement. Still, I
have to admit that I do feel some responsibility for Paul's
part in the affair. But to come back to your remark, I
should imagine that Ewan would find an extended loan

from a brother-in-law a very acceptable solution to his worries. And that is how I would approach the subject—*after* you and I were safely married, of course. And he probably wouidn't pay too much attention to the whys and wherefores; he'll simply think I saw you again, found you as irresistible as ever and swept you off your feet, fortuitously solving his problems on the way.'

His smile mocked her as he lifted the latch. 'Only we two would know the truth.' He paused. 'So it's up to you. Think it over, Rosamund. On the other hand, of course, you could pray for a miracle,' he added with heavy sarcasm.

'Get out,' she breathed. 'I wish I had never——'

He lifted an authoritative hand. 'Careful, my sweet,' he said smoothly. 'As I see it, there are only two options open to you, and I might even withdraw mine if I were sufficiently provoked. So don't burn your boats yet. I'll give you twelve hours. You know my home telephone number. If you haven't phoned your acceptance by ten o'clock tomorrow, then—well, we can only allow events to take their sordid course, can't we?' He stood looking at her for a moment, and she stared back furiously. Then he said softly, 'You've had your hair cut. I like it. It gives you the look of a medieval page—hauntingly different.'

'Please...just *go*... I don't give a damn what——'

He closed the door firmly behind him as Roz stumbled back to the sofa on legs that felt oddly boneless and insubstantial.

For a time she sat staring at the closed door, as if Nick's silhouette had been carved on it. Pressing tightly clenched fists against her cold, strained face, she willed herself to think. Think! But she was stunned, completely stupefied by tonight's turn of events. This kind of thing didn't happen in real life, her brain kept repeating. Not these days, and certainly not to someone like herself: reserved, self-contained, even unadventurous. As Ewan had remarked, she was the *strong* one—a distinctly unappetising description. But it was true enough. Even from an early age she seemed to attract responsibilities.

Resolutely she tried to shake herself free from such pointless meandering, and absently picked up the doll she had been working on. Even that seemed more real than this evening's events.

Her knowledge and expertise in her craft had been built up slowly, out of hours spent standing in draughty auction rooms or in stifling summer marquees. Visits to museums and exhibitions and hours of research in libraries had expanded her knowledge. And all her hard work was beginning to pay off. Clients were trusting her with commissions to hunt out rarities; only the previous week she had tracked down a Georgian doll's house for a delighted collector. And now, people who were tiring of stripped pine furniture were seeking out chairs and chests painted in the colours and decorative styles of their origins. That was a new and lucrative market. She enjoyed her work, finding it an absorbing and demanding challenge. *This* is my life, she thought numbly... *This* is reality.

There had been other men in her life since her affair with Nick ended: men who were attracted by her pale skin, the too-prominent cheekbones, the generous mouth and eyes which met their own frankly without coquettishness. But after three or four dates she found their sensual intensity bored her—as anything did unless one could share it. Sometimes she made herself face the fact that Nick had spoiled her for other men. Or perhaps, she reflected, she carried the drive for perfection in her work into more personal areas and had become too selective. And at such moments she had to remind herself that perfection in human nature didn't exist. Or, if it did, it would be uncomfortable to live with. And, anyway, who was she to demand perfection in others?

And after such analysis she would turn back to her work with relief. With that, she knew *exactly* where she stood. Dolls couldn't hurt or deceive or lie...

And now Nick had stormed back into her life with his preposterous solution to Ewan's troubles. Ewan... He would probably come over soon, ready to tell her about Nick's visit, and wanting to know what Nick had said to her. The bright white light in the workshop would be merciless, and her face might reveal too much that mustn't be told. Better if she went back to the house where the soft lighting could conceal...

Ewan was slumped in a chair staring moodily into the fire. He looked up, saw her in the doorway and grimaced. 'Sorry, Roz. I told Nick you would be busy, but he brushed that aside. What did he have to say?'

She managed a careless shrug. 'Oh, we just talked a while, that's all. The point is what he said to *you*.'

Ewan gave a low whistle. 'It was all very uncomfortable and humiliating. He talked to me like a Dutch uncle, as if I were a child. Pointed out the errors of my ways and so on. For two pins I would have taken a swing at him and told him to get out. But I wasn't in a position to attack.' He gave a regretful smile. 'Strictly speaking, Nick's only concern should have been with my debt to Paul. But he's a shrewd operator. Before I knew what was happening I was telling him the whole story, even itemising every damned sum I owe.'

'Did he tell you what might happen if—if you can't find the money?' Roz said.

'He didn't have to. My imagination has already done that. Roz,' Ewan stood up suddenly, his face almost unrecognisable in its lines of stress, 'what the hell am I going to do?' He stared round wildly, as if seeking an escape route.

Roz went over to him and put a hand on his arm. 'Try to put it out of your mind tonight,' she said tonelessly. 'We can do nothing right now, and worrying isn't going to help. Try to get some sleep, then tomorrow we'll address the problem, as they say.' She produced a tiny laugh as she pressed his arm. 'Somehow we'll find a way out of it.'

But Ewan wasn't listening. 'I sometimes think,' he said dully, 'that when Lisa died it was as if—as if the tide went out. For me. And now I don't think it's ever going to come in again.' He kissed her forehead with lips which were alarmingly cold. 'Bed it is, then. But—sleep? I doubt it.'

She listened to his footsteps on the stairs, then she dropped into a chair. The sight of him walking away like an old man hurt too deeply for the tears which had been threatening ever since Nick left. And those words about the tide going out... A strange remark from a brother whose devil-may-care insouciance she had once envied.

Lisa's death had changed everything, she thought miserably. Not only for Ewan, but for herself. And, whether she liked it or not, she had no choice but to consider Nick's offer, at least. She couldn't watch Ewan suffer, and this was only the beginning. Besides, she had promised their mother...

She closed her eyes. So many painful memories tonight, threads from the past weaving the pattern of the present...

Roz alone had known the seriousness of their mother's illness and the tragic prognosis. She had given up her job as secretary to a local veterinary surgeon in order to be at home during those last months. On fine days she had driven her mother out into the green dales which they both loved; they had walked a little, watched waterfalls, talked, grown close. On bad days she and her mother had dressed dolls for charity shops. That was the origin of her present work. But then it had been simply a means of making her mother feel useful, a kind of therapy.

Somehow Ewan had sensed Roz's heartbreak and the reason for it. In his own clumsy fashion he had tried to help: a bowl of daffodils one day when she had been unable to conceal her tears, take-away meals brought in, congealing in their cartons, to save her the trouble of cooking.

Then, towards the end, her mother had said, 'You will keep an eye on Ewan, won't you? He's a darling son, but——' she had smiled, her ravaged face lighting up for a moment '—so like his father. He needs a woman to keep his feet on the ground sometimes.'

Remembering unlocked the tears, and Roz laid her head on the arm of the chair and gave in to them. When she finally wiped her eyes some time later she felt drained of everything except the one resolve that she had to help Ewan in the only way open to her.

She glanced at the clock, surprised to see that it wasn't yet eleven. Squaring slim shoulders, she went briskly to the telephone. The sooner it was over, the better. She didn't have to look up the number of Meronthorpe; like so much else connected with Nick, it was engraved on her memory.

He answered the call, and if he was surprised by her quick decision his voice revealed nothing. She had expected some positive reaction, but his tone was laconic. 'Fine,' he said. 'We'd better talk about it and get things perfectly clear. I have to go away tomorrow evening, so I'll be round to see you in the morning. Ten-thirty, say?'

In the dull fatalism of Roz's decision, a little grit of independence hardened. If she had to take this step, then by heaven she would at least have some say in the pace of it. 'Not tomorrow morning,' she said curtly. 'I'll be busy. I'll expect you at two-thirty.'

'One-thirty,' he said, and hung up.

She resisted an impulse to smash down the receiver. Heavens above, this was only the beginning! What had she done? But what else *could* she do in the circumstances?

There was a lot to think about, and her brain was racing. She got into bed remembering Ewan's observation that Nick was a shrewd operator. He was used to getting his own way, to manipulating people, and Roz guessed that tomorrow's meeting would be loaded with controversy. She didn't trust him one inch, and if necessary she must be prepared to fight for certain conditions.

She took a notepad and pen from her handbag and began to list the points she intended to raise. Like an agenda for a meeting, she thought, feeling the earlier hysterical laughter threaten to rise again in her throat. A paper marriage! But her own interests must be protected. Nick wasn't going to have everything his own way!

CHAPTER THREE

Roz must have slept eventually, for she awoke in her usual mood of optimism before the memory of the previous evening dropped like a curtain of rain blotting out a blue sky. For one panic-stricken moment she was aghast at what she had done. She must have been mad! Then her common sense reasserted itself, doggedly telling her that she had no option. And, in view of the news which she would have to give Ewan soon, it would be sensible to prepare the ground. He must never suspect the real reason for the marriage.

He was halving a grapefruit when she went into the kitchen. Dark smudges beneath his eyes told of his sleepless night, but Roz didn't remark on them. Instead she said lightly, 'It was strange seeing Nick again after so long. He was telling me about Martel Leisurelife—that's his company. He's certainly dynamic.'

'Oh?' Ewan stared at her vaguely. 'He wasn't commiserating with you, then? Wasn't telling you what a damn fool brother you've got, and so on?'

'Of course not. We talked about our work mostly. He seemed quite impressed by my achievements. You know,' she went on confidingly, 'I think he's changed. Of course, it's two years since we saw each other... Anyway, he seemed quite—interested. He's coming over to see me this afternoon.' She bent over the toastrack to hide her hot face. Deception was nasty, and this was only the beginning.

But she had captured Ewan's attention. 'You do surprise me. I thought you didn't much care for him.'

Roz shrugged. 'We-ell, we drifted apart, but that's a long time ago, and it's silly to let the past prejudice the present—and the future, isn't it? Life's too short.'

'Well, you certainly look bright-eyed and bushy-tailed,' said Ewan grudgingly, 'and anything that pleases you pleases me.' He stood up, taking a last swallow of coffee. 'I'll be off, then. Have fun.' He went out, moving as if he dreaded the day ahead. You and me both, she thought, with a sinking heart.

The minutes until lunchtime seemed to crawl, each one a drip building inexorably into a frozen mass where her stomach should be. But after midday time flew frighteningly fast. You're being pathetic, she told herself bracingly. This is a business arrangement from which Ewan, and therefore yourself, can only benefit. Forget Nick's motives. Without this deal, Ewan would have to sell his printing-design consultancy, Grey Garth would have to go, all her stock... She would have to go back to secretarial work, live in a cramped flat... As for Ewan, the loss of his business and his home, coming so soon after Lisa's death, would finish him.

Roz shook her head impatiently; she would *not* go into all that again. It led nowhere; she had made her decision and must be positive about it. The coral wool dress she took from her wardrobe was a crutch for her spirits, as were the high-heeled court shoes and the blusher she stroked over her pale cheeks. After living so much of her life in jumpsuits and slacks, neat tweed or flannel suits and silk shirts, she felt unusually feminine as she studied her reflection. Trust Nick to bring out that side of her! She sprayed her throat with the last drops of Joy, closing her eyes sensuously as the drift of perfume reached her nostrils. If she had to go down before the onslaught of Nick's go-getting personality, then it would be with all flags flying! No more pathos, bathos, she scolded herself, no more——

The doorbell rang. She jumped, then, squaring her shoulders, she went down, her eyes apprehensive.

Nick stared at her speculatively, as if assessing her changed appearance, then he held out a paper-wrapped sheaf. 'For you,' he said, coming into the hall. Immediately the scents of spring came in with him, and Roz buried her face in the bouquet of cool irises and freesia, hiding her smile of pleasure. Then she glanced up at him. His face was politely blank, no smile, no golden warmth in his eyes. His whole ambience was that of the clear-cut, well-tailored tycoon, here to grind out yet another business deal.

'Thank you,' she said stiltedly, dropping the flowers carelessly on to the hall table. 'I'll see to them later. I take it you won't be staying long.' The flowers were simply his idea of doing things properly, she realised, her lip curling. And, of course, that was the way the whole deal would be made to appear: proper and conventional.

She took his light cashmere coat and led him into the sitting-room where the firelight vied with a shaft of thin April sunshine that slanted through the old leaded lights.

'Perhaps we had better come straight to the point,' he said brusquely. 'I have a plane to catch.'

'Why, of course,' She raised clear eyebrows in surprise. 'I've no intention of detaining you one moment longer than necessary.'

'Good.' He sat down, glancing quickly at his watch. 'First. Our marriage will take place fairly soon. All right with you? I can give my secretary all the tedious details and leave it to her. It'll spare you the trouble of trying to look suitably dewy-eyed. Shall we say, the third week in May? I'm fairly free then.'

'How overpoweringly romantic,' Roz murmured caustically, her mouth twisting.

Nick's eyebrows flicked up. 'As I recall it, romance doesn't enter into our agreement. That ended two years ago. To resume—I'd thought a quiet wedding breakfast afterwards at Meronthorpe. It would please my father. You can leave all that to me. How many guests do you intend inviting?'

This conversation was assuming the qualities of a nightmare, Roz thought, getting up to go and stand by the window. 'You mean—how many of my friends would I like to witness the—the travesty?' She wondered if she could go through with it, but remembering her earlier resolution she forced herself to turn and face him, her expression composed. 'I think,' she said carefully, 'the quieter the better. Just Ewan.'

'Right,' Nick said tersely. 'Ewan on your side, Paul on mine.' He allowed a flicker of humour to slide over his austere features, smoothing out the lines that seemed to have developed running from his nostrils to the corners of his mobile mouth. Were those lines there last night? Roz wondered distractedly. 'Just the interested parties, one might say,' he added drily. 'And a honeymoon in Venice. Is that agreeable?'

Roz gritted her teeth, wondering if he had also made an agenda for this meeting. He dealt with each point succinctly and economically, as if mentally ticking them off before moving on.

'Honeymoon?' she queried. 'Is that really necessary in the circumstances?'

He leaned back in the chair, regarding her through narrowed eyes, and she recognised the latent power of his body, the muscled strength that the well-cut suit couldn't hush. 'Ah,' he said thoughtfully, 'the implication worries you, does it? Yes, certainly a honeymoon is necessary. This is going to have all the trappings of an orthodox marriage. And if it's romance you're missing,' he added slyly, 'then just think how romantic it will *seem*.'

'Will it? I don't quite follow.'

'Of course it will,' he said impatiently. 'A reconciliation after two years, a whirlwind love-affair, followed by the most private and intimate of weddings. Then a couple of weeks in Venice.' He paused as she stared at him suspiciously. 'In separate rooms, of course.'

'That's a relief,' Roz snapped, angered by the brusque efficiency of his methods. He seemed to have everything under control. Hadn't he any feelings at all? Even regrets that this whole thing was a blatant mockery?

'And afterwards,' she said, her lips stiff, 'where will we live?'

'At Meronthorpe, of course.' He seemed surprised that she should ask. 'You'll be company for my father. Even if he recovers from his stroke, he probably won't be very mobile.'

'Really?' She stared at him, meeting his gaze coldly. 'Naturally I'm very sorry about your father, but I didn't realise that was part of the arrangement. Or is it by way of being a bonus for you?'

He frowned. 'I don't follow your line of thought, my dear.'

'I'm sure you do,' she retorted. 'I wasn't aware that you were also looking for an unpaid nurse and companion for your invalid father.'

'I'm not. He's already got one, a Mrs Fellowes. Salaried.'

'Then in that case there's no reason why I should live at Meronthorpe. I prefer to stay here. I intend to carry on with my work, and my present arrangements suit me.'

She faced him defiantly. The thought of leading some empty kind of life at Meronthorpe where, each time he came home, they would have to promote the lie of a loving marriage, was just too much!

'Very well,' he said after a moment, 'Grey Garth will be our home. For the time being,' he added darkly.

'For at least two years,' she insisted. She didn't quite know why she had imposed that particular term. Maybe it was because two years seemed to be a significant time factor in her life. And perhaps, an inner voice suggested hopefully, within two years Nick might give her grounds for divorce. That could be her only hope for the future. 'And about Ewan's debts?' she asked, pressing her advantage.

'They will be settled immediately we're married. He will then owe *me*.' Nick smiled creamily. 'So if you have any intention of welshing on your part of the bargain after it's signed and sealed, I'll be down on him before your dust has settled.'

Roz's eyes blazed a black fire. 'You've got it all worked out, haven't you?' she breathed.

'Naturally. As, apparently, you have. Now, shall we move on? Your—shall we say, *duties*? I shall expect you to be hostess to my guests whenever the occasion arises, to accompany me when I think it desirable, and just generally to behave like a devoted wife. In return, I'm shouldering your brother's debts, and I shall make you a generous allowance.'

'I don't want your charity,' she snapped. 'I have my work.'

'Of course. I was forgetting.' He dismissed her skills with an apparent contempt that infuriated her. 'I don't think you'll find it *too* difficult to honour your commitments.'

'Nicely put,' she scoffed. 'And now I'll tell you what *I* expect, shall I?' Her breath was coming fast and angrily, and it took an effort to control her rage, but it was vitally important that she appear as cool and hard-headed as he was. 'I shall expect courtesy and consideration at all times. Not just when others are around.

And,' she added pointedly, 'if you have to play, then you play—away. I'm sure you understand my meaning.'

To her surprise he laughed, the notes ringing out heartily in the crisis-charged room, as if she had said something witty.

'It's crystal-clear,' he nodded, 'and of course I'll comply. As for the courtesy bit—you'll have to earn it, won't you?' His voice hardened suddenly, and with another glance at his watch he stood up.

Roz felt as if she had been through a millrace, tossed and buffeted along a dangerous channel. Nick looked quite unperturbed, as if this whole situation was a trivial matter. Suddenly she wanted to hammer her fists against that broad chest, just for the satisfaction of seeing his face register some gut emotion, even anger.

He stood for a moment looking down at her. 'Well, I think we've just about covered the most important details. It's all quite simple, really. A verbal contract between two people.' He turned to go, then came back towards her. 'Oh, one more thing. Visit my father sometimes. Will you do that? He always liked you, you know.'

After a moment she nodded. Visiting his father would be the easy bit.

'Good.' He reached into an inside pocket and took out a sealed envelope. 'While we're on the subject, get yourself some wedding finery some time. It's a blank cheque. But I'd like to see the receipts.'

'You don't trust me, do you?' she whispered, taking a step towards him.

He reached out to cup her chin between a hard forefinger and thumb, jerking her face up. 'I trust you as much as you trust me,' he said. 'Past experience showed me that you were a creature of impulse, and it's not beyond the bounds of possibility that you might spend some of that money on your brother.'

Violently she shook her head free. 'Whatever else Ewan might be, he's not a sponger,' she flashed.

'No? Well, perhaps I judge him too harshly,' said Nick. 'But it does appear to me that he's got off very lightly. He's fortunate in having a sister who ——'

'If you think he isn't beside himself with worry,' she began, 'then——'

'Worry?' Nick's eyebrows lifted, and he gave a short bark of laughter. 'We all have worries, but we usually deal with them ourselves. I shall be away for two weeks. I'll write to you, of course, and when I come back we'll have to see a great deal of each other.'

'I follow,' Roz said wearily. 'You mean we have to set the scene.'

'That's right. You shouldn't find it too hard. After all, you have quite a talent for deception. You certainly deceived me.'

'Despite your wide experience of women?' Roz said waspishly.

'Quite. Now I must go.'

She watched him walk towards the door. She would have given anything to throw the envelope after him and tell him that the deal was off, but his mention of Ewan was probably calculated to remind her that she had no choice. Woodenly she followed him into the hall.

'Just one more thing,' he said as he shrugged into his coat. 'I take it that you're not into any romantic attachment at the moment? Nothing—*heavy*?' he emphasised. 'But—no, I was forgetting. You don't go in for heavy relationships, do you?' His body tensed suddenly and his hands came out to pinion her arms to her sides. 'Because, damn you,' he ground out, 'I will *not* be made a fool of again.'

'You don't have to tell me that,' she retorted, adding silently, You're the one with the talent for making fools of people. Just as you did with me—once. But not again.

Oh, no. I learned my lesson the hard way, but learn it
I did.

'So long as we know where we stand.' His voice had
reverted to bland pleasantness. 'And do take that look
of baffled fury off your face, my dear. This is one of
the happiest days in a woman's life, I'm told.'

With a low laugh of mockery he closed the door softly
behind him and was gone, leaving Roz choked by a
furious frustration.

She wished that the Sloots were in residence in their
part of the old house. She needed someone to talk to.
Not about Nick; she would never be able to confide in
anyone the real reason for her marriage. But pleasant
domestic chatter would at least smooth a veneer of normality over the rest of the day. But Anna and Piet were
in Holland.

However, she had her dolls, and with a resigned
grimace she changed into working clothes and went over
to the stable. By late afternoon she began to feel that
she was coming to terms with the future. She even found
a crumb of consolation in the fact that Nick spent so
much time away. So it could be worse. She made herself
repeat the words at intervals during the afternoon, deliberately reaching for optimism. And, as she would still
be living and working here, marriage wouldn't make such
a vast difference—only in the sense of a loss of freedom
that was Ewan's gain. And that was the important part.
Determinedly brainwashing herself, she gradually found
what comfort she could, and by the time she heard
Ewan's car in the drive she was able to open the door
to him, showing the kind of expression which might pass
for happiness, provided he didn't look too closely. And
he wouldn't, of course, she told herself; he would be too
preoccupied by his own troubles.

He sniffed appreciatively. 'Lamb with rosemary,' he
remarked. 'Who are the flowers from?'

'Nick, of course. I told you he was popping in.'

'You're—not picking up the threads?' Ewan looked surprised. 'Don't tell me that my misdemeanours have brought you two together again.'

Roz forced a laugh and poured him a sherry. 'It's a bit early for that kind of speculation. Oh, I don't know, though . . .' Her smile was as tight as an outgrown skin, and inside she felt slightly sickened. She would be glad when the acting could stop. Then she realised with a sudden plunge of her spirits that it never would—in the foreseeable future, anyway.

'Well,' Ewan raised his glass to his lips and smiled thinly, 'I just hope I'm around to watch the love-affair blossom.'

Just in time, Roz stopped herself from completely re-assuring him. Instead she said, 'Look on the bright side. Your creditors aren't yet beating the door down. We'll find a way out of it. Now I must see to the joint.' Humming happily, she went into the kitchen.

But maintaining a false front was a strain, and after the meal she went up to her room, closing the door with hands that quivered with a life of their own. This had been quite the worst day of her life, and she felt sick with deceit. She had committed the worst kind of be-trayal, the violation of her own integrity. And for two men! She should hate them both! The self-consolation that she had snatched at during the day drained away. But she couldn't hate Ewan. As for Nick . . . her mind shuddered away from making any kind of rational judgement while depression numbed her senses.

Yet, once, he had been everything she had wanted . . .

She got up from the bed and went to her dressing-table, dabbing her aching forehead with eau-de-Cologne, hating her wretched, despairing reflection in the mirror.

How she had loved him! Once. He had seemed to hold the key to her essential being. With him, all her niggling little responsibilities receded; she had somehow expanded, opening like a flower to the sun. Everything, just everything, was more vivid when Nick was around. And there were the little things, unimportant in themselves, but revelations at the time. Like the way she would telephone him to tell him something, only to hear that he was on the point of calling her for exactly the same reason. And there were his kisses, which aroused a deep longing that pulsated through her long after the kiss had ended.

His past hadn't mattered. In any case, she had argued silently, his exploits were probably grossly exaggerated by village gossip, or mere sour grapes from women who were attracted to him. She ignored the veiled warnings. What if Nick *had* been a 'rakehell', as one woman termed it? Virile, good-looking, prosperous enough to indulge his desires, it was inevitable that he would attract attention. His so-called misdemeanours she attributed to his appetite for life. And, anyway, they had belonged to the past and the days before Ilona's party.

That year, as her twenty-fourth birthday approached, Roz had the feeling that the occasion would be very special; everything seemed so ripe with promise...

Nick had had to go to Birmingham on business the previous day, but would be back in time for them to dine at the country club on her birthday. Roz was stepping out of a long, luxurious bath when the telephone rang. He was full of apologies, but some business had come up unexpectedly. He sounded so distraught that it hadn't occurred to her to doubt him.

She was disappointed but understanding, and philosophically she had hung away the gauzy silver dress bought for the occasion to put on slacks and a jacket. At the time she was looking after a friend's dog, and rather than spend the evening moping she had taken it for a walk across the fields to the next village, wondering if Nick would be back in time to call in at Grey Garth so that at least they might have a birthday drink together.

Roz was coming out of the bridle-path when she saw his silver Mercedes parked in the yard of the Packhorse Inn. At first she couldn't believe it. He was in Birmingham, wasn't he? She quickened her footsteps, her heart leaping. He must have cancelled the appointment and rushed back. He would be having a quick drink to relax, and then...

Then she saw that the car wasn't empty. He was there, but not alone. She froze, then shrank into the shelter of a hawthorn. Paralysed with disbelief she saw his sudden movement, watched his hand move up to touch long blonde hair beside him, then draw a girl's head down on to his shoulder. It was a gesture Roz knew so well that she almost felt the gentle pressure of his hand against her own head. Then he bent, and his face was hidden...

Sobbing with shock, she turned blindly and stumbled home, impervious to the snatching claws of bramble that fringed the path, the ruts and ridges worn in the ground by a thousand hoofs. All her hopes, the joys of the past months, had been flushed away. She felt emptied, almost as if she had bled to death.

Village gossip flooded back, amplified now. She saw faces, well-meaning or malevolent. 'Playing with fire...' 'My goodness, I could tell you some tales about the parties at Meronthorpe. They had to call the police in one night, I remember...'

On and on went the voices, filling the emptiness, replacing the love that had been wrenched out of her by the realisation that he had lied to her. He was her first and only lover. Why, only two nights previously... No! something shouted inside her. Don't think about that night!

Fortunately Ewan hadn't known how far her relationship with Nick had progressed. Because of his initial disapproval at Christmas, Roz had deliberately avoided the mention of specific names when she went out in the evenings.

When Ewan came in that night he found Roz staring at an old film on television. 'Thought you had a date?' he said, surprised.

'I did, but you know how it goes. Something came up and he had to cancel.' Roz bent to sweep some ash from the hearth, hiding her face.

'What a rotten way to spend a birthday. If I had known, you could have joined Lisa and me.' He swung round suddenly. 'It wasn't—Martel, was it?'

'Why do you ask? What makes you think that?' Roz stalled, staring at the neat heap of ash.

'No. No, it couldn't have been him. I called in at the Packhorse earlier and saw him there with a blonde. He didn't see me. He was too engrossed.'

So now, in place of that impossible trust was a deeply rooted suspicion and the humiliation of having allowed herself to fall for his obvious charms. And all the while he was probably laughing at her naïveté.

Well, he wouldn't find her naïve now. She felt older than Eve, and she would cope with this grotesque marriage somehow.

But tonight, after such a day, her memory seemed incapable of burying the past. She had telephoned him the morning after her birthday.

His voice had held its usual warmth as he'd said, 'Hello, darling.' Warmth? Or had it been merely a bluff and hearty cover for his real feelings? She had had to steel herself against tears, deafening herself to the inflexions and smoky sexuality of his deep voice. Never would she let him know how vulnerable she had been.

She hadn't let him get beyond the greeting before she cut in. 'I've been thinking things over, Nick, and I've come to the conclusion that we're being a bit silly. And—well, the fact is, things are beginning to get too intense for my liking.'

At first he had been astounded. 'Is this a fit of pique because I had to break our birthday date?' he demanded. 'I couldn't get out of it, and——'

But she didn't want his explanation, although it might have been of academic interest to discover how he would explain away that kiss in the car. But it would have been all lies. The truth was the scene Roz had witnessed; he was with another woman outside the Packhorse when he was supposed to be in Birmingham.

'My birthday?' She managed a tinkle of laughter. 'Oh, that wasn't important. And you don't have to explain,' she hurried on. 'That proves my point exactly. We're both free agents, and I realise that I'm not into heavy relationships. And I think perhaps it would be better if we didn't see each other again. Sorry if I unintentionally led you to believe otherwise, but it's better that I lay my cards on the table now rather than let things drift on.'

'*Drift?*' he roared. 'We never *drifted*. We made music together, and you know it. Why, only two nights ago we . . . What the hell's got into you? I'm coming round. Right away.'

She closed her eyes, suffused by a feeling of utter bone-weariness; all her strength had been channelled into her voice. 'It's no use,' she said shortly. 'My mind's made up. Let's just leave things. Anyway, I'm off to stay with a friend and I'm just about to go. I arranged it yesterday,' she lied. 'I don't know when I'll be back.'

There was a silence, and then he said ominously, 'I see. Are you——?' But she hung up before he could say any more.

When she came back she learned that Nick had gone to Florida. No doubt when he didn't receive a reply to his letter he realised that she meant what she said.

She threw herself into her work. When any mention was made of the Martels, she would compose her face and pretend only a passing interest. Occasionally she caught sight of Nick at a distance, sometimes with a group of friends, at other times with a girl, and never the same one twice, and she would congratulate herself on having had a narrow escape. Had their love-affair lasted any longer her heartbreak would have been proportionately greater.

Well, all that was behind her now. Ahead was a future she had been trapped into by Ewan's recklessness.

Nick's letters came, brief, curt messages which meant nothing; only his handwriting on the envelope, for Ewan to notice, gave them some conventional importance.

When he came home they went out together, in public preserving a front of perfect harmony. When he helped her on with her coat, or took her arm, she tried not to shrink from him. Her nerves felt as taut as violin strings, her heart had ceased to be a living organ, merely a lump of cold, barren metal. There were times when she knew she couldn't go through with it. And then she would think of Ewan and his habitually harrowed expression as he contemplated an uncertain future.

Fortunately Nick was away quite a lot, but as her wedding day approached she felt that, in one sense, it would be a relief to get it over and done with. Then at least the gloom would lift from Ewan's face. As for herself, she doggedly tried to live each day as it came and not to think about a future utterly bereft of promise.

CHAPTER FOUR

THROUGHOUT those weeks Nick's cheque had lain in a drawer in Roz's room like something obscene, belonging only to darkness. He had bought her at a price which released Ewan from the immediate pressure of his debts, and Roz had accepted that. But this personal gift seemed to spell out the message too emphatically, rubbing her nose in it.

And yet, her treadmill brain argued, wasn't the situation sensitive enough, without her making it worse by refusing the money? Also, she was fully aware that Nick's life-style demanded certain standards. He liked his women to be well-dressed, she remembered, with a little downward turn of her mouth.

Her own bank account was perilously low after the last spate of doll-buying, and one thing was sure, she couldn't turn up at her own wedding wearing some snappy little number from a chain store.

With an exclamation of impatience at her indecision, she took out the cheque, staring at the bold signature for a moment, then she tucked it into her wallet. Maybe expensive and stylish clothes might give her a kind of Dutch courage, an illusion of well-being that would last long enough to see her through the parody of her wedding day.

But as she dressed for the wedding, even the pure silk stockings and expensive gossamer undies failed to lift her spirits. And, as she adjusted the little ivory-coloured bowler on her smooth, glossy bob, the fact that it was the perfect partner to the Italian silk suit was wasted.

With eyes dulled by misery she stared at her mirrored reflection, seeing the lovely clothes as simply the glamorous gift-wrappings of an empty box.

She was to remember very little of the ceremony, only her own coldness and the violent tremors that seized her, and her grudging gratitude for the support of Nick's arm, even as inwardly she cringed from the proprietorial gesture.

When he turned to kiss her under the beaming approval of Paul and, to a lesser degree, Ewan, she gritted her teeth stubbornly and held herself rigid in his arms, waiting only for the kiss to stop, while inside her desperation mounted. As Nick stood back from her he was smiling, but his eyes held a cold, yellow glint, and she felt a flicker of satisfaction that his lips had felt the rebuff on her own. If revenge was his game, then she, too, could play.

The wedding breakfast had been prepared in the huge master bedroom at Meronthorpe. Rolfe Martel awaited them, propped against pillows on an antique day-bed, meticulously shaved and groomed, and wearing a crimson brocade robe with a velvet collar. Roz thought that he looked a little like Oscar Wilde, his appearance lending authenticity to the bizarre situation.

Rolfe's stroke had been severe enough to affect some movements, but impaired his speech only slightly. As Roz bent to kiss his cool, dry cheek, he gestured with his eyes to the chair drawn up beside him. 'Be off, Nick,' he murmured, looking beyond Roz. 'I want to talk to my daughter-in-law.' He gave a slightly twisted smile. 'I know this is supposed to be *your* day, my dear,' he said, 'but it's also mine. This is the first time in many years that I've entertained a lovely young lady in my room. Takes me back a bit. And besides, a wedding breakfast here in this damned prison is like a breath of fresh air.'

Roz, saddened by the change in his brusque, astringent manner which she had once found a little daunting, took his hand and said, 'Let me bring you something to eat. How about the lobster?'

'I doubt if I can manage it.' Then his eyes, so much like Nick's but without the golden glints, twinkled. 'But perhaps you could feed me?'

Roz laughed. 'Are you making a pass at me?' she asked.

He pressed her hand. 'I would prefer to call it flirting— a much prettier expression. Yes, I suppose I am. And why not? I imagine that son of mine flirts with you, and why should he have all the fun? It's the icing on the cake, the meaningless song that lifts the heart, and— oh, lord, here comes my keeper!'

Roz glanced up to see Mrs Fellowes approaching, smiling pleasantly, to offer her good wishes. Roz smiled back. She had taken an immediate liking to the older woman when Nick had brought her to Meronthorpe three weeks ago.

'Away with you, woman,' said Rolfe, and turned back to Roz. 'Beneath that smiling exterior,' he confided, 'beats the heart of a monster. She makes me do exercises, would you believe?'

Roz exchanged a laugh with Mrs Fellowes. This light-hearted banter was a welcome antidote to the tension she felt when Nick was close. 'I should think so, too,' she said stoutly. 'So would I if I had the thankless job of looking after you.'

At that moment Nick joined them, his expression approving his father's raised spirits.

Rolfe's eyes twinkled. 'Tyrants, both of you,' he grumbled. 'I don't know who's going to suffer most— me or Nick. "Monstrous regiment of women." Now, who said that?'

'Wasn't it John Knox?' Roz laughed.

Nick was grinning. 'There now, Father, didn't you always say that Rosamund was the brightest of all the girls I brought here?'

Just in time, Roz bit back the obvious retort and stood up, but Nick slid his hand around her waist, drawing her to him with a slight pressure. She stiffened, sensing that it was a warning. 'All right, darling?' he asked easily. 'Now, come and have some food or the kitchen staff will be most disappointed.'

'I was just about to get some for Rolfe. He wants me to feed him. Isn't that right, Rolfe?'

'Oh, but Mrs Fellowes will do that, won't you, Nancy?' Nick interposed. His voice was pleasant enough, but his grip had tightened meaningfully.

'Now look what you've done, Nick,' exclaimed Rolfe. 'Roz and I were getting along fine until you two broke things up.' He looked from Nick to Nancy Fellowes.

'Don't excite yourself, old man,' Nick laughed. 'You'll be seeing plenty of my Rosamund. But today I want my bride to myself. Heaven knows,' he added, with a quizzical glance at Roz, 'I've waited two years for this day.'

It was a convincing act, Roz decided, suggesting as it did that he had carried a torch for her since the morning they broke up. Masterfully he tucked her arm in his, drawing her close to his side as he led her over to the table. The feel of his thigh brushing hers and the warmth of his body against her hand brought a blush that heated every nerve in her. 'Now, do try to look as if I'm the only man in the world, will you?' he murmured silkily. 'This won't last much longer. In another half-hour we can be on our way. Try to remember our bargain, Rosamund.'

The smooth menace of his words replaced the warm blush with a prickling coldness. 'Am I likely to forget?' she breathed bitterly.

Then there was the toast and Nick's short speech that said all the right things. Somehow Ewan and Paul had found an opportunity to hang signs and boots and tin cans on the back of the Mercedes, and Nick and Roz drove away with all the panoply of a conventional wedding send-off.

'I'll stop at the end of the drive,' Nick told her, 'and get rid of all this junk. Well? Don't you think it went off smoothly, all things considered?'

Roz didn't answer. She closed her eyes, leaning back into her seat. She felt spent and desolate at the thought that there could be no going back. Instead she was tied to this man for the foreseeable future. He owned her; she was his vassal, he the overlord. Her tension had hardened into a blinding headache, and her brain seemed ready to explode into fragments.

Nick dropped a light hand on to her knee and she flinched. Immediately he withdrew his hand, and his voice had an edge of steel as he said, 'Apart from looking a little pale, you put up quite a creditable performance.'

She shot a sideways glance at him, noting the tightened jaw, and she knew that her shrinking away had angered him. Well, he would have to get used to that!

'Thank you,' she said coldly. 'So long as you realise that it *was* just that—a performance. But right now I'm off-stage. There isn't an audience and I've got a headache.'

'Poor darling,' Nick murmured sarcastically. But he slid a cassette into the player and, apart from the soft, soothing music, they drove to the airport in silence as Roz feigned sleep.

Venice was everything that Roz had expected, and more. Nick had reserved a suite in one of the *palazzo* hotels overlooking the Grand Canal, and for a few moments they stood on the balcony of the richly furnished salon that connected their separate bedrooms, staring across the water, mesmerised by its soft slap-slap against the weedy green stones opposite. Roz felt strangely soothed, so that even the nightmare circumstances of being with Nick seemed subdued by the ancient beauty around them.

'Let's change into something more comfortable,' Nick suggested. 'Then we'll take a look around. That is, if you feel up to it.' Roz guessed that he suspected her headache of being a ploy to withdraw from him and isolate herself.

She looked at him stonily. 'Oh, I don't intend to miss one little thing of the *world outside*,' she said. Venice might be the epitome of romance—something which would be lacking in her life for a long time to come— but she intended to concentrate on the positive side. It was the only way. And what better place to begin?

In her own room she hung away the suit and threw the hat into a cupboard, knowing that she would never want to wear either of them again.

Nick had changed into honey-coloured trousers and a casual black silk shirt. He looked somehow warmer, more human, she thought with a slight shock. He was no longer the clipped, hard-mouthed partner in a soulless contract, and his appearance now flooded her with sudden, shy apprehension. She asked no more than the ability to tolerate his presence on a level of indifference; but now, with a sinking heart, she had the first glimmerings that it might not be that easy. His personality was far too invasive for mere stony tolerance. Too much charisma, she thought, looking away from him quickly. It seemed to assail her; and too much of a past they had shared still haunted her like an old perfume.

'Shall we do all the tourist things?' he said, taking her arm as they went into the Piazza San Marco. His touch scalded her bare arm, and she tried to withdraw it, but his hold tightened. 'For pete's sake, relax, girl,' he gritted.

They sat outside Florian's, sipping drinks. An orchestra had set up its stands and was playing a lilting Rossini overture. They watched the *passagiato*—the throng who, in the cool of the evening, emerged to stroll and exchange greetings and look in windows at exquisite jewellery and glass, to sip a drink outside one of the cafés and watch the world go by. The crowd moved in an ever-changing pattern: beautiful, nubile Venetian girls, sometimes with plump, elegant parents, pigeons insatiably importuning a crowd of Bermuda-shorted Americans, and dark, earnest Japanese, clicking cameras.

As Roz sipped her martini she was silent, her eyes alight. She did not want to miss one nuance of the marvel of being part of this scene in what was surely the loveliest city in the world. Nick, too, was silent, and for that she was grateful. His recent caustic manner could distort a scene which she wanted to remember for as long as she lived.

Then, inexplicably, out of nowhere came a memory of damp, green Yorkshire dales, impinging incredibly upon the pink and white stones, the blue and gold exoticism around her; a recollection of many other moments when her thoughts and Nick's had dovetailed, fitting perfectly together as one intrinsic piece. And she realised that, at this very moment, Nick understood exactly how she felt about Venice! He was silent out of consideration for her mood.

She flashed him a quick, startled glance and knew that he had been watching her face. 'Thank you, Nick,' she murmured involuntarily before she could stop herself, knowing that instinctively he would understand.

He made a negating movement of his hand. 'Shall we go? It will still be here tomorrow.'

The intimacy was dispelled. Thank heaven for that. Another couple of moments, and in spite of herself she might have dropped her guard. He had hurt her enough two years ago; there would be no repeat performance.

They dined on the terrace of their hotel, watching the light drain from the sky into sugared-almond colours of misty green, pink-flushed grey, hazy mauve. But the meal held no pleasure for Roz, for she was unable to stem the flow of memories of other meals they had shared, sometimes forking food from each other's plates, laughing, touching each other, leaning forward to kiss, Nick moving a vase of flowers out of the way so that he could take her hand, erotically stroking her palm and arousing delicious sensations.

If only... she thought, oh, if only they could have put back the clock to the time when an occasion such as this evening—their wedding evening—had seemed the inevitable climax to their love-affair.

But there could be no going back. They were no longer the same two people. And the past was dead and must be buried, she told herself sharply, taking a sip of her Orvieto.

And now there was the night ahead... Almost here... Were separate rooms any deterrent to a man like Nick? And she hadn't even noticed if there was a key in the lock of her room. Suddenly the whole business of getting herself to bed seemed beset with pitfalls.

'You're not eating much,' Nick remarked, breaking the uneasy silence. 'Headache still bothering you? Surely not.'

'What?' She started as his voice shattered her preoccupation. 'Oh, well, yes... it is a little.'

'Then we'll get something for it. I suppose it *has* been quite a day.' His eyes were deceptively languid as he gazed at her, and she wondered if he saw through her pretence. It *had* been quite a day. Was his remark innocent? Or could he be hinting that it was going to be quite a night? Or was she simply being neurotic? She swallowed nervously, wishing that she could read his mind. And was it always going to be like this—herself on the defensive, wondering what, if anything, might lie behind his remarks? How could she know when to trust and when to mistrust?

She pushed her chair back suddenly, scraping it harshly over the tessellated marble floor. 'I think, if you don't mind, I'll go up now,' she said. 'I'm really very tired.'

He rose politely. 'Perhaps that would be best. I'll finish my cigar before I come up. And,' he went on abrasively, confirming her suspicion that even her thoughts didn't escape his notice, 'don't worry, my dear. I don't have sex on my mind all the time.'

She gasped at his frankness, her face colouring. 'I should hope not,' she snapped. 'And I'm sure it isn't necessary for me to remind you of your part in our—bargain.'

'I know, I know,' he murmured, maddeningly nonchalant, 'business only. And I never mix sex with business. So don't worry, fair Rosamund, you're quite safe.' He drew on his cigar, adding sneakily, softly, 'So if sex is on anyone's mind, I would say it's on yours. *Buonanotte, cara mia.*'

She swung away quickly, trying to compose herself, and his soft laughter followed her. But in spite of his reassurance she locked her door with a satisfying sense of security.

She undressed swiftly and was in and out of the bathroom within five minutes. Brushing her hair a few moments later, she heard a tap on her bedroom door. She froze, breath held, brush poised. It seemed that, even out there, he must surely hear the thunder of her heart. 'Rosamund?' he called softly. Then, with wide, horrified eyes, she watched as the gilt knob turned slowly, almost stealthily. Hypnotised, she stared, knowing herself to be safe, yet not believing it. There was a thick, waiting silence as she imagined him standing there, head tilted, listening. Then a moment later she heard the quiet click as he closed the door to his own room. She sank down on the bed, expelling her breath in a long, shuddering sigh. So much for *his* integrity!

Trembling, she got into bed, that gentle tap echoing through her head. So, for all his fine words, sex *had* been on his mind. Why else would he come to her door? She had the answer now to her earlier question: she could *never* trust him one little millimetre!

She closed her eyes, burying her head in the pillow and trying to exclude all thoughts of him. But he had played such a significant part in her life recently that his image seemed burned into her mind, and again she was gripped by the most poignant of all the memories she had tried so hard to obliterate.

She recalled that other dinner, far away, two nights before her twenty-fourth birthday. Everything had been perfect, and afterwards she had asked him back to Grey Garth for coffee. 'I won't stay late,' Nick had said. 'I've got to get off to Birmingham first thing tomorrow, but I'll be back the following day—your birthday.'

Her eyes had shone as she passed him his drink. 'You remembered!' she had teased. 'I hope you haven't bought me soap. Ewan always does. Do you suppose he's trying to tell me something?'

Nick laughed. 'That would be too subtle for Ewan. Where is he, by the way?'

'He went up to Edinburgh on business. He'll be back tomorrow, I expect,' Roz said vaguely. 'And must I wait? Won't you give me even the tiniest hint?'

Nick put his cup down and reached for her. 'Mercenary creature,' he murmured, his breath against her ear fanning the thrill of his nearness. 'The only thing I will say is—I hope it will change our lives.' His lips sought hers and she turned to him with an upsurge of love, her hands pulling down his head to hold his mouth against hers until they were both breathless.

'Rosamund...oh...' he whispered, his voice thick and unsteady. 'I want you, every inch, every pore...' His hands moved to cup her breasts, then slid upwards to ease down the thin straps of her dress. His finger-touch seemed to heat her skin, drawing each nerve into a sensitive awareness that her needs matched his. She gazed up at him, her eyes wide, an exquisite tremor shivering within her. He stood up, then bent and gently picked her up. 'Which way?' he said hoarsely.

And then she was lying on her bed, the moonlight making a lattice pattern on the duvet.

Lovemaking was uncharted territory for her. She wanted him so much, yet she wondered if the experience might be marred by her ignorance, her half-fearful reservations. Supposing he was disappointed? Supposing they were in some way physically incompatible? What did she know about her own body?

But, as if he understood her agony, he kissed her again. Gently at first, then with an increasing passion that swept all other thoughts out of her mind. Tenderly he undressed her, lingering over each separate garment, kissing the skin he had uncovered, arousing her to fever pitch and yet managing to control his own desires. His lips brushed her breasts, took her nipples and teased them into buds of ecstatic hunger, his hands stroking the silky skin of her inner thighs. Her body was awakened into an instrument of delight, capable of giving and taking an even higher pleasure, until at last she found the waiting unbearable. With a groan he took her, his body a living flame, his shudders dominating the rhythm of her movements, sweeping her along with him into an explosion of passion that left her spent and weeping with joy.

And much later, as the dawn was breaking over the hills, it had been just as magical, but quite different. Gently and persuasively he had taught her how to get pleasure from pleasing him, revealing small, delicious intimacies she had never dreamed of... A morning of mornings, she had thought, bemused and enchanted.

When he left, his kiss bruised her, his hands crushed her. 'The next time it happens, I don't want to have to say goodbye in the morning,' he said harshly, his eyes holding hers in a clasp that seemed almost physical.

Well, Roz thought, coming back to the present and pounding her hot pillow, noticing that it was wet with tears, full marks to Nick for showing her the depths of her passion. He had taught her so much about *herself*; and the following day she had learned the truth about *him*. Perhaps he got a kick out of seducing virgins. Perhaps that was what had appealed to him; she had presented a challenge which, once met, had lost its value. But, perversely, he couldn't now forgive her for ending the relationship. Damn him, she sobbed silently. Damn him and the way he can get to me, even now, when it all ended two years ago.

She got up and poured herself a glass of orange juice from the crystal jug on her bedside-table, then with a little thump she set the glass down. This wasn't the way to handle the present situation, behaving like some silly, weak, sex-hungry woman wallowing in a past love-affair that events had proved wasn't the monumentally wonderful thing she had thought it to be at the time.

Nick was starting his breakfast when she went into the adjoining room the following morning. He looked up, smiling impersonally. 'Good morning. You've been very quiet. I didn't think you were awake yet. And fully dressed, too! Perhaps I should have waited.'

In the ancient room furnished with ornate antiques, he struck a note of vibrant modernity, clad only in a pearl-grey robe with discreet yellow piping. His legs were bare, and Roz sensed that, underneath, he was naked. Coming so soon after her tormented night, the thought made heat rise treacherously in the pit of her stomach and she turned away.

She had deliberately left her diaphanous négligé over a chair. Buying it had been a mere sop to the conventional idea of a trousseau, and now, in baggy jade-green slacks and a matching striped top, she felt herself to be safely camouflaged.

She gave him a thin smile and sat down. 'There's enough here for two,' she said. 'I'll ring for another cup.'

'What a tiny appetite you have,' he quipped lightly. 'Not in love, are you?'

When she didn't bother to answer, he went on, still in the same easy tone, 'You must have slept very well and almost immediately. I knocked on your door last night, but the silence was deafening.'

She glanced up, startled. She hadn't expected him to refer to his frustrated errand. There was an ironic glint in his eyes as he lounged in his chair. 'I got you that aspirin,' he explained lazily, 'from the night porter. But it seems I needn't have bothered.'

'Oh . . . well, thank you for the thought, anyway,' she faltered, dropping her napkin and bending to retrieve it, in the hope that the movement would cover her confusion. So *that* was why he'd come to her door! Or was it? Perhaps he'd had another motive.

'And now something tells me that you don't believe me.' His eyes narrowed in amusement, the skin at the corners of his eyes fanning into crinkles. 'You must think you're the world's most irresistible woman. Such vanity, my dear!' His gaze held hers in a sparkling golden clamp. 'You're lovely, Rosamund,' he said softly. 'I don't deny that. But I've never yet had to force my way into any woman's bed, and I don't intent to start now. You of all people should know that. And, in any case, I'm a man of my word.'

Oh, yes? Her eyes asked the silent question. Then you must have changed...

'Also,' he said curtly, 'I recollect that you don't welcome heavy relationships, so I doubt if we would be much good together. Even though we were once.'

Roz stared at him stonily. So that was how he summed up that night at Grey Garth! Just two people in bed being 'good together.'

'Well, I won't deny I'm relieved to hear it,' she said stiffly.

'So the precaution of locking your door last night was superfluous. And now that we've cleared the air I'll get dressed, and then—the Doges' Palace, Santa Maria della Salute...?'

'Whatever you say,' she answered. 'I'm in your hands.'

He gave an amused laugh and went to his room.

Sunny, golden days blended into each other. Beauty and artistry spread an endless mosaic before them as they tirelessly explored the wonders of Venice. At night, exhausted, Roz slept soundly.

Nick was a stimulating companion, ready and avid to move from one place to another, to learn the story behind the shape of the gondola's prow, to stare bemused at paintings, his face lit by a consuming interest that shared itself with Roz's eagerness to see, to feel, to experience—everything, even the narrow streets, *calles*, with their peeling stucco and dark, mysterious doorways that were almost sinister.

On the ninth evening Nick said thoughtfully, 'There's one thing we haven't done yet.'

'Oh?' Roz put down her drink and pushed her hair back. She felt tired yet relaxed. The sun had given her a warm tan, and she knew a sense of utter well-being. She seemed to have successfully put the past behind her; perhaps that night of weeping had been a catharsis. And in all honesty she had to admit that Nick was the perfect companion. Now she was able to grin at him and say, pertly, 'And what's that?'

'We haven't been in a gondola yet. And that's something every tourist should do. So come on, let's go.'

They sat side by side on the cushioned seat, watching the economical strokes of the gondolier in his wide-brimmed hat. Slowly they glided past ancient palaces with fretted stonework, beneath bridges into tiny, secret canals. It seemed a world apart: the green water, the sky fading to a lilac haze, the distant echo of footsteps over unseen stones.

'I'll never forget all this,' Roz murmured. 'It defies description. You would expect it to be somehow—spoiled, eroded, because...' She shrugged helplessly, unable to find the right words.

'You're talking about an overkill?' Nick suggested, smiling.

'Yes, that's it exactly. I mean, it's been painted...'

'And written about,' Nick agreed. 'Shakespeare——'

'Yes. And Thomas Mann... That wonderful Visconti film——'

'Not to mention the Christie and Sutherland one. And, before you were born, they were doing it. Hepburn and Brazzi...' Nick screwed up his eyes, thoughtfully watching the movements of the gondolier. 'And let's not forget the music—Gilbert and Sullivan had a go.'

Roz looked at him and began to laugh out of sheer elation. Then she felt his arm around her shoulders, and she stiffened. 'Relax, Rosamund,' he breathed, his voice handling her name in the old, heart-stopping way. 'Whoever heard of a man and a woman in a gondola sitting as if they had just had an almighty row?'

His warm palm on her thinly covered shoulder was a fire under her skin, and she had to fight the betrayal of her senses. This evening everything—the mood, the scene, the leisurely drifting motion—seemed to conspire against her determination to be purely practical. She had guessed that there would be moments like this when his touch would still hold magic for her. But past experience had shown how worthless such moments really were. Rolfe had spoken about the icing on the cake. Perhaps that was what this was; only there was nothing so substantial as cake. Simply icing.

In a sense she could equate it with Venice itself: a fairytale city built on marshes. But who, seeing it, thought of the mud beneath? It was enough to be grateful for what stood above the water and to enjoy it all.

Perhaps that was the right approach to Nick's magnetism. She heard her breath go out in a long sigh, and she leaned against him, giving herself up to the combined spell of the historic place and the modern man— Nick. His hold tightened fractionally. 'We only need music now,' she murmured.

'But there is music. Listen.' And she heard the strains of a mandolin coming from the terrace of a small, vinehung restaurant. 'There'll be dancing there later.' Nick said. 'Shall we go?'

Roz's sense of enchantment mounted as she bathed and dressed. Her severely cut white dress accentuated her tan. The long jet ear-rings swung against her slender neck, adding a touch of drama and echoing the dark sparkle of her eyes. She stood before Nick, lifting her arms and twirling slowly. 'Like it?' she asked softly.

For a moment he watched her in silence, the lambency of his eyes at once flattering and disturbing, and she had her answer.

The terrace under the vines was lamp-lit and intimate, the central dance-floor little larger than a billiard table. With three other couples, dancing was out of the question. They could only hold each other dangerously close, swaying, hardly moving while a trio played the melodious, romantic music of the country.

The last of Roz's half-hearted resistance melted. The gondola ride has suspended the resolutions which she had clung to like a lifeline, and now, with Nick's body close to hers, it was as if the past two years had dissolved in a time warp, and the future didn't exist. Time in Venice was time out of life. What a crime it would be to waste it and not to respond to the sensual glamour—the icing.

Her hands clasped at the back of his neck and she closed her eyes, letting her body lean into his, feeling his cheek against her hair, breathing the faint, masculine scent of his body cologne. She was too absorbed in sensation to talk much. Only the senses ruled tonight: the sound of the mandolin, the persuasive thrill of his body moving against hers, the taste of the wine on her tongue... Total enchantment, she let herself be steeped in it.

They stayed until the restaurant had closed and the trio were starting to pack away their instruments. Then, under a star-hung sky, they walked slowly back to their hotel, sharing the night with a few late revellers and the sinuous shapes of the cats.

Once in their own sitting-room Roz kicked off her shoes. The symbolism of the act struck her keenly, like a cold wind; the dancing-shoes discarded, the evening was over. Oh, but she wasn't ready for it to end. Not yet. And not like this, with the distance between them bafflingly reasserting itself now that the romantic interlude was over.

'Nick——' she began hesitantly. Then stopped. What was there to say?

He was throwing his jacket over one of the brocade chairs and turned quickly. There was a watchful intensity in his face, and his eyes seemed to pierce her to the core. 'Yes?' His voice came sharply.

'Oh...nothing, really. But—thank you for a lovely evening.' She heard her voice take on a conventionally polite tone, lengthening the distance with each word.

Nick went to a cabinet and poured himself a whisky. 'Join me?' he said. As she shook her head, shuddering, he said blandly, 'I enjoyed the evening, too. Thank *you*.'

'Well,' she began uncertainly, 'it's been a long day...'

'Yes, it certainly has.'

'So I think I'll go to bed. Goodnight.'

Feeling curiously let down, Roz went into her own room. She didn't lock the door, knowing that, more than anything, she wanted him here beside her tonight, whatever the future held. Surely he must know? He was quick enough to tune in to the more acrimonious thoughts she harboured about him. So surely he... She lay awake, listening, hoping, longing... Then at last she fell asleep, resigned to the knowledge that he would not come. Either he did not want her, seeing her only as a contract wife, or he was, indeed, a man of his word—*now*. Or could it be, a little niggling voice urged, that this was part of her punishment for walking out on him two years ago? How it must have rankled.

Just before she slept she had a preview of their marriage, a bleak, unsatisfactory relationship which must bear all the obvious marks of success. It looked as if it was going to be even more difficult than she had imagined.

CHAPTER FIVE

MORNING brought sanity, throwing cold water on Roz's feelings and desires of the previous night, and reviving the truth of their situation. She must have been mad! It had all been part of the spell woven by this incredible place, moonlight on the water, romantic music; in short, the icing, and nothing more.

She saw that Nick had breakfasted early. 'I've got quite a lot of telephone calls to make,' he told her, 'so why not go shopping?' He took out his wallet and passed her a bundle of notes.

She recoiled quickly, shaking her head and draining her coffee-cup. 'No, I'd rather not.'

'Why? What's the matter?' he drawled softly, his eyes narrowing speculatively. 'Do you think my money is tainted?' There was a twist of amusement on his lips.

In some strange way she knew that the distance between them had widened. Or could it simply be that it had taken the falseness of the previous evening to illuminate the reality? she asked herself. While Nick had appeared happy to go along with the romantic mood of the evening, he had later succeeded in making it perfectly clear that he had no desire for her. He had bought a wife, a social asset—not a woman to love. And the fact that he hadn't wanted her stung what little vanity she had—even though now, in the clear light of morning, she realised that if he *had* come to her room last night she would have hated both him and herself afterwards, but particularly herself for capitulating to the . . . the lust of the flesh. Lust . . . what an ugly word. Like *tainted*.

72

'Don't be silly,' she said with a brittle laugh. 'It's just that there's nothing that I particularly want to buy.'

'Really?' he marvelled. 'Yet I could swear to have heard you enthuse in front of almost every shop window we've passed. Oh, for pity's sake,' he snapped suddenly, 'don't be so squeamish, Rosamund. You're going to have to get used to spending my money, so you——'

She jumped up, her eyes snapping. 'Why? So that you can feel big? Powerful? The great provider? Is it that you want me to feel obliged to you for every penny you put my way? And while we're on the subject, in case you hadn't noticed I'm not cast in the mould of some of your girlfriends——'

'What exactly is that supposed to mean?' he asked very softly.

'Must I spell it out? I'm speaking of those girls who find your money an irresistible inducement to have an affair with you.'

She didn't know what had prompted her to be so vituperative; she was surprised at her own fury, and she knew that she had gone too far. His skin strained whitely against the hard jaw, and there was a vulpine glint in his eyes. But she couldn't stop herself. 'What a blow that must have been to your vanity, Nick. Or didn't you ever guess what lay behind the ease of your—your conquests?'

'Oh, I guessed,' he gritted, flinging down his pen. He stood up, towering over her in silent, angry menace so that Roz shrank back. But his hands reached for her shoulders and roughly he pulled her towards him. 'And now let me spell out something to *you*, Rosamund. What right have you to denigrate those other women, when the whole basis of our situation is your need of money and my ability to supply it?'

'That's unfair.' She winced under the pressure of his fingers. 'At least I never pretended. I didn't scheme and flatter you, and I——'

'No, you certainly didn't! Instead you behave as if I were contaminated and you're afraid of it touching you.'

Irrationally Roz felt tears gather. Where had the closeness of the past days gone? 'I'm sorry,' she said tightly. 'It's just that you—you're so...' She compressed her lips, fighting down the temptation to weep. 'Look, Nick, I too have a business. Oh, *you* don't consider it much, but it is mine. And it will provide me with—with spending money. I don't need any handouts, and I think——'

He stared down at her, his face obdurate, his mouth set in a line of sheer male strength. 'And *I* think you've over-reacted. Now, I wonder why? You sound almost neurotic, Rosamund,' he said icily. 'Let's get one thing straight, shall we? You're my wife, right? Oh——' he released her shoulder to wave a dismissive hand '—I concede that it's in name only. But that is the only reservation, understand? So don't try to deal in high principles with me. Your business can provide you with whatever it will. That has absolutely nothing to do with me. But as your husband I would expect you to have some share in the money I make, also. Have you got that?'

'Oh, yes, I've got it, loud and clear,' she retorted. 'A good, old-fashioned marriage where the husband is the boss. It gives you a gratifying feeling of superiority, just as I said.' He gave an impatient grunt, but she hurried on. 'Well, just listen to me for a moment. I had no option but to marry you. But it might surprise you to learn that I'm not too happy about a situation which forces me to see myself as a kept woman. Isn't that what I am?' Her face flamed. She needed to escape from his presence, which seemed to diminish her. 'After all, you're keeping the roof of Grey Garth over my head, putting food in my mouth. I have to—to accept all that.' Her voice broke a little, but she pushed herself on. 'But as for the—the gifts and the goodies, you can save those for—for—other women. I assume that I *am* permitted some small say in matters? Is that so unreasonable? And right now I choose not to spend your money. It's as simple as that.'

'Simple? I see.' He gave her a long, considering look. 'Yes, I see it all. You're still trying to hold on to your independence. But in case you haven't noticed, my dear, it's a little late to think of that now.'

She felt the heat ride high into her face, prickling her scalp. But inside she was cold and shaken. 'We *did* agree not to interfere in each other's lives,' she began, 'and naturally——'

'And *this* is interference? My giving you a few miserable *lire*? For pity's sake, Rosamund, be your age!' he thundered, suddenly at the farthest limits of his patience, accompanying each word by a little shake. Then, before she could guess his intention, he bent his head swiftly, his mouth sealing her trembling lips, stopping any further argument. His lips felt hot and dry, almost feverish. They burned her mouth as if he were branding her as his own possession, searing his own private mark deep into her flesh. Not a kiss, she thought, recoiling inwardly. Simply a purely male macho gesture. But already her mouth was beginning to throb under the assault, and she felt herself grow weak.

She tore her head away, panting. 'How dare you?' she breathed. 'How dare you add insult to injury with such a—a...' She was trembling inside, and suddenly speechless. She could see the white patches at the corners of his mouth, the two lines that ran from his nostrils deeply incised. She twisted violently out of his grasp, her breasts rising and falling with each outraged, shuddering breath. 'You're—despicable!' she spat.

'You had better go,' he answered, with sudden bitterness. 'I've got these phone calls to make. I'll see you later.' He dropped the money disdainfully on to a marble-topped console table.

She glared at him for a moment, her eyes stormy, then she turned on her heel and left the room, dashing the money to the floor as she passed.

She almost ran through the foyer and into the street, as if to escape from Nick and all that he represented in her life.

She walked for two hours, randomly, along back-water canals, over small bridges and through narrow *calles* opening into tiny squares. At first she saw nothing. There *was* nothing—only the scalding frenzy of her blood, the noisy, ugly clamour in her head.

Then, later, suddenly spent, she found a café and ordered a *cappuccino*. What a thoroughly nasty scene it had been! How had it started? And why? In honesty, she had to admit that she had gone over the top, taunting him with the mention of other girlfriends. That must have hurt him. But she had *wanted* to hurt him! To punish him for . . . for not—for not wanting to make love to her? She winced. Oh, no! She closed her eyes, suddenly sickened by the implication. Once Nick had brought out the best in her; now he seemed to bring out the very worst.

She stared miserably into space, not even noticing the interested glances of two lithe young Italian men at an adjacent table. Yes, Nick had been right; she *had* over-reacted, using his generosity as an excuse to vent her frustration. After all, he had always been generous, and perhaps for him *not* to have offered her some spending money would have been totally out of character.

And yet there had been more than a grain of truth in her angry outburst, she assured herself doggedly. She *did* have the right to refuse; heavens above, she had to have some freedom of choice, otherwise their life together was going to be hell. And he hadn't actually *bought* her, she told herself firmly, although perhaps that was the way he saw things. In which case, it was more than ever essential that she settled that point straight away.

But what a way of doing things! A blazing row, a clash of personalities that left her still reeling from the impact.

Wearily she got up and made her way slowly back to the hotel, quailing at the thought of facing him again.

He was sitting on the balcony drinking a large Campari and soda. He turned as he heard her footsteps. His face bore no sign of the ravages of his earlier rage. He was probably able to dismiss that quarrel as if it had never happened, she thought numbly. Perhaps to him it had no importance, whereas for her... 'I'm glad you're back,' he said equably. 'I'm sorry to cut short this idyllic honeymoon,' he went on with a tiny nip of sarcasm in his tone, 'but I'm afraid we have to leave. I've got to go back to Bermuda. Some business has come up in connection with a property deal.'

Dully she sank down beside him. 'I see.' For the moment she felt too drained and tired to register any disappointment. 'Would you—like me to pack your clothes? Like the dutiful wife I must be?'

'Is that an olive branch you're offering?' He raised a quizzical eyebrow, then when she didn't answer he shrugged. 'No, thank you, my dear. I'm used to quick getaways. I can pack for myself.'

Blindly she nodded, then said quickly, in a small, desperate voice, 'Nick, I'm sorry that I—went berserk this morning.' She stared down at her hands clenched in her lap, then glanced up at him, her eyes earnest and imploring. 'But you must—you simply must—allow me to make some decisions for myself.'

Laconically he lifted his glass, squinting at the light through the rosy liquid. 'The trouble with you,

Rosamund,' he said after a moment, with slow deliberation, 'is that you're used to making *all* the decisions.'

She stared at him, her eyes frosting defensively. 'That sounds rather profound. What does it mean?'

'Isn't it obvious? Since your mother died you've had all the worry of Grey Garth. You helped Ewan to set up in business—oh, yes, my dear, I know the part you played in that. I, too, hear some of the local gossip.' He shot her a spiky glance, a reference to her earlier taunt which he had no doubt guessed stemmed from the same source. 'Then you got your own business off the ground. And now, to top it all, this latest problem—Ewan's debts—was also laid at your door.'

She watched him warily. 'It looks as if you have given the subject of—me—some thought,' she said quietly. 'And what you're really saying is that I've grown hard.'

'What I'm really saying is that you've changed since your twenty-fourth birthday,' he murmured. 'That was when I last knew you. Or thought I did. But you weren't—hard last night, Rosamund. You were—delightful. And you enjoyed it, too. Perhaps you should try a little harder to develop that side of yourself, hmm?' Again the eyebrow lifted teasingly.

But Roz frowned. He really had a nerve! she thought. To bring up that particular birthday, for any changes in her since that time originated in his behaviour then! She stood up, smoothing down her blue linen skirt busily. 'I'm sorry that the changes in me don't meet with your approval, Nick,' she said coldly, 'but life has a way of shaping us all. And you can't have it both ways, you know. Only a woman with some degree of—of resilience would have been able to marry you on these terms. Now I'd better go and pack.'

She was surprised to see her fingers trembling slightly as she folded her clothes neatly into the suitcase. Nick's words had cut her to the quick. And he was right, of course; she had had to keep her feet well and truly on the ground in order to survive. That was the hand that life had dealt her, and Ewan's gentle, drifting nature had slipped all the decisions neatly into her lap. Not that she was complaining...

She brushed a weary hand over her hot forehead. But sometimes, just occasionally, it would have been good to have someone to lean on; someone with whom she could simply let go, respond to in a soft and feminine way. She thought that she had found that person once, in Nick, but she had been utterly wrong.

And now he had the bare-faced audacity to criticise! She tried to stir up her anger against him, but couldn't. She knew that his thoughtful, perceptive words would linger far longer in her memory than the quarrel of this morning.

In the bathroom she splashed her face with cold water, then went into the sitting-room. Through the open door she could see Nick's bed. His suitcase was open, and he was deftly packing. 'Sure you don't need any help?' she called, anxious now to put the acrimony of the morning behind her.

'Quite sure, thanks. We've got time for an early lunch, by the way.'

'I'm not hungry,' she said, and went to stand on the balcony to watch a *vaporetto* chug busily past. This had surely been the most bizarre of honeymoons; storms and sensitivities all laid bare... But there had been another side to it, too, she reminded herself, determined to be honest. Friendship and common interests, sudden mellowing of the atmosphere between them, Nick's magnetism...

He came to stand beside her. 'Taking a last look?' he asked softly.

She nodded, afraid to speak because of the pressure of tears in her throat. With all her heart she wanted to turn her head into his chest, feel his arms around her. But a rebuff would be more than she could bear at this moment. 'We *do* have to go, I suppose?' she asked tremulously.

'I'm afraid so,' Nick said. 'And I had lined up a day in Verona, and a performance of *La Traviata*. But that's the way it goes, Rosamund,' he added ruefully. 'Business, you know. Sometimes it can be a dirty word.'

She turned away before he could sense her tears. Business. Yes, that said it all.

Grey Garth seemed chilled and drab after the colours and soft light of Venice. Even the kitchen looked sterile and uninhabited and unfamiliar. Roz frowned. Ewan wasn't the tidiest person to have around the house, and his cup and saucer, at least, should have been in evidence, along with a few empty beer cans. Pricked by a sudden needle of alarm, she ran up to his room. His one formal suit was missing from his wardrobe, and his suitcase had gone. As she passed the window, she noticed that the Sloots' car was parked in the drive next door. They might know where Ewan was.

A few moments later Anna Sloot drew Roz into the house. 'Ewan? A business trip, he said,' she told Roz. 'He will be back tomorrow evening. But why are you here? Ewan said that you wouldn't be home until——' Her grey eyes sparkled, lively and interested. 'But what is all this? The so-secret wedding? And where is the husband? You will dine with us so we all meet this evening. *Ja?*' She laughed, a warm, rich chuckle. 'There is plenty for four. Piet says that I am the big enemy of his waistline. So you will come—with this mysterious husband?'

Her gaiety was infectious now that Roz's worry about Ewan was removed. 'We-ell,' Roz started, a little shyly, 'the wedding was rather sudden. And thank you for the invitation, Anna, but...may I let you know? I'm not quite sure if Nick has something planned for this evening.'

'Just come. Turn up, as you say, if you can. In about half an hour?'

Roz thanked her again and went slowly back to her own front door. It was possible that Nick might wish to go over to Meronthorpe to see his father tonight. Her eyes clouded; despite his stroke, Rolfe's eyes were sharp, and in his inactive life he would have plenty of time to speculate about this marriage. Under his scrutiny she would have to be very careful.

Nick was in the room adjoining her own, putting away the clothes which had been brought over by a servant during their absence in Venice. Roz leaned against the door-jamb, watching him. 'By the way, we've been invited next door for dinner tonight. But I've paved the way for a refusal,' she added. 'I thought you might want to go over and see your father.' Carefully she averted her eyes from the single bed, but even so it seemed to impinge upon her vision, a silent reminder of this hollow union.

Nick straightened. 'Which would *you* prefer?'

'I'm beginning to learn not to make all the decisions,' Roz said sweetly. 'This one's yours.'

He looked at her for a long moment, a half-smile on his lips. 'You remembered,' he murmured. 'Oh, I think we'll go next door. Might as well meet the neighbours and satisfy their curiosity. I'll call in and see Father tomorrow on my way to the airport. Unless,' he added, his voice dropping to a low, suggestive purr, 'you would prefer to dine *chez nous*. Just the two of us, here. An extension of our honeymoon?'

'Not at all,' answered Roz impassively.

'Good. Then that's settled. The sooner we start meeting people together, the sooner you'll perfect your act.'

'I've acquitted myself well enough so far, haven't I?' said Roz acidly. 'Incidentally, what did you do about Ewan?'

'Ewan?' Nick's mobile eyebrows lifted. 'Oh, you mean his debts. I transferred a nice round sum into his bank account, and unless he's more stupid than I supposed, he'll have paid off every cent he owes by now.'

'Why must you be so—so derogatory about him?' Roz demanded. 'Is it completely beyond your understanding to appreciate how he got into this mess?' Nick's sardonic expression goaded her on. 'After all, didn't his—*stupidity*, as you term it, get you a wife? A business asset? An image-enhancer? Not to mention a means to pay off old scores. It's certainly what you said you wanted before we were married. Or could it be,' she went on scathingly, 'that things haven't turned out quite as you had hoped?'

His amused laugh stung her. 'I try not to deal in hopes too often,' he said indifferently. 'Plans, intentions—yes. Hopes—only rarely.' He hung up the last tie and stood perfectly still, watching her. 'Did you think I had hoped for—more? That I *wanted* more from you? Your body? Your loving?'

She glared at him. 'I don't know what you want,' she breathed. 'And I don't care very much.'

'Good,' he said indifferently. 'We both knew that it wouldn't be roses all the way, but I hope that you're not warming up for another quarrel. I don't think that would be a good idea just at the moment. You used not to be so aggressive. What time are your Dutch friends expecting us?'

'Just about now,' she retorted. She went into her own room, closing the door firmly between them. Was it true that she had once loved him to the extent where her life and her thoughts had been centred only upon him? He had a talent for angering her as no one else ever had. She beat her fists together in a sudden spasm of frustration. Thank heaven he was off to Bermuda tomorrow. For two weeks she would be free to resume her own life as if she were still Roz Parrish, not Mrs Dominic Martel.

She showered quickly and was slipping a pearl-grey silk dress over her head when Nick opened the communicating door, dressed and ready. The faint woody scent of his cologne reached her in a breath-catching intrusion, taking her unawares. 'Not quite ready?' he said. 'Then I'll wait here, if I may. Besides, you're going to need a hand.' He smiled smoothly at her rebellious face. 'With your zipper, of course. Turn around. You see, Rosamund, we husbands do have our uses. Anything else I can do for you?'

'Nothing at all,' she said spikily.

'Pity.' He gave a resigned shrug of perfectly tailored shoulders. 'Oh, in case you hadn't noticed, there are a couple of messages for you on the telephone-pad. "Ring Brad Williams." And again, "Ring Brad W immediately," heavily underlined.' Nick sat down on the stool, leaning one elbow on the edge of the dressing-table, looking at her enquiringly. 'Just who is Brad Williams?'

'A friend,' she said tartly, clipping on coral ear-rings.

'Might I ask what kind of—friend?' His voice was soft, but there was something almost threatening in its lack of expression.

'Certainly you may ask. How detailed a definition would you like? He's a man friend, obviously, and I do business with him sometimes. It happens, you know, in my line of work.'

'And that's all? Just business?' Nick shot out. 'Because we're not playing games with this marriage of ours.'

'No, we're certainly not,' she retorted. '"Games" suggests pleasantness, diversion, *enjoyment*.' She glared at him. 'You really do believe you've bought me, don't you? Body and soul.'

'Body?' he drawled, his eyebrows lifting above amused topaz eyes. 'How you do harp on sex, my darling. As for the soul part, that's altogether too metaphysical for me. I stick to the substance. What are you doing?'

Roz had unclipped her ear-rings and tossed them down on to the dressing-table. 'If you think' she breathed disjointedly, 'that I'm going next door to see my friends with you in this mood, you can—think again. Get out of my room. I'll tell Anna that I've—got a headache—or something. Just go!'

'Another headache,' he murmured, sarcastically sympathetic. 'I recall that you had a headache on our wedding day. A refuge, is it, perhaps?' His lip curled as he stood up, then he reached for her. 'Whether you like it or not, you can put these ear-rings on again.' He dropped them into her hand. 'You're not getting out of this dinner engagement. *I* made this decision, remember? So try to look pleasant, Rosamund. Take my arm—like this.' He threaded her arm through his, pulling her closely to his side. 'Introduce me to your friends as if you know you're the luckiest girl in the world. And smile. Defer to me occasionally, and——'

'Go to hell,' she whispered. 'Don't touch me. Who *are* you to—disrupt my life like this? To just walk in and turn everything... Making me feel...'

'You're being incoherent again,' he said sweepingly. 'And you know very well who I am. Your husband. And your friends will have preconceived notions of how a man and wife, just back from honeymoon, behave towards each other. There should be a certain...*glow*. We mustn't disappoint them, must we?'

She compressed her lips tightly; whatever she said would only be twisted to his advantage.

'So, just for starters——' he said, his voice dropping seductively. His hand slid smoothly over the silk of her dress, coming to rest on the middle of her spine. With his other hand he turned her to face him. She scowled at him, but the deep compulsion of his gaze insidiously quelled her rebellion. This was the face of the man she had once loved, the face she had often touched, exploring with sensuous pleasure the strong bone structure, the sweep of russet eyebrows, the curving mould of well-defined lips. Those days were gone, yet their memory still flavoured her life. The bright loathing faded from her dark eyes, her lips softened in sad acceptance of the inevitable.

And, as if he saw the gentler line of her pain, he bent his head quickly. His lips dusted hers with a lingering sweetness that melted the frustration that made her body and mind a battleground armoured against him. She was helpless, drowning... Not even wanting to be saved. A tiny sigh like a broken thread escaped her, but it was caught up and gathered by his mouth as the kiss strengthened to a blind, driving force which made her writhe in his arms as the first exquisite thrill rose inside her. She knew—hadn't she always known?—why no other man had attracted her since she had put Nick out of her life. The familiar room receded, the dinner engagement was forgotten. There was nothing else in the world that mattered, but this, the increasing heat of his mouth, the honeying of her resistance to him. Her lips parted invitingly as her hand went up to his face.

But he put her from him gently. 'Time to go,' he said. She stared up at him, baffled. He seemed quite composed, almost untouched, while within herself needs and desires clamoured for satisfaction. 'Now is the best time to go,' he said softly. 'On a high note.' He turned to open the door and stood aside as she passed through in a daze, unable to think straight.

Still in a daze she made the introductions and watched the evening develop. As she had expected, Nick rose to the occasion, and only once or twice did Anna's obvious curiosity about the sudden marriage shadow the easy conversation. But Nick guided it away with the skill of a mountaineer bypassing a crevasse.

'That was a wonderful meal,' he said at last, putting down the red napkin that matched the candles on the table. 'And what a lovely home you've made here. I've always thought that the Dutch excelled at marquetry, and that table is a perfect example.'

'You must take a closer look at it,' Anna said, smiling. 'It's quite—remarkable. Is that the right word?'

'Certainly.' Nick laughed down at her, and Roz could see that he had made a great impression on Anna. Not that Piet would mind: he had monopolised Roz's attention from the start.

They moved into the other room for coffee, and talk became more general. Roz sank back into the feather cushions of the big curved sofa. If was hard to believe that only twelve hours ago she had been in Venice.

Through drowsily narrowed eyes she watched Nick as she sipped her coffee, listening for his laugh, unwillingly respecting his far-ranging knowledge when the conversation turned to Dutch holiday complexes. She was deeply aware of him there, sitting across the room from her. The fine grey suit, and the ease with which he wore all his clothes, blended sophistication with a carelessness that stemmed from a root of confident, virile masculinity. She shivered suddenly. As he handed her the refilled cup their fingers touched for a moment, making a powerful connection. She recognised it as a signal to her deepest, most feminine sensors. As with alcohol, she reflected weakly, one couldn't remain entirely immune to its effect. She caught him watching her, and she made herself smile and turn to Anna with a remark about the flower arrangement in the corner.

It was obvious now that Nick was a hit with the Sloots. And Roz, too, was relieved that the evening was a great success, thanks largely to him. Yet as they said their goodnights and Nick put an arm around her waist to draw her against his side in a natural, familiar gesture, she found herself stiffening. Everything seemed to go *his* way, she thought, with a trace of bitterness. He was always the victor, never the vanquished. He seemed to know better than anyone else just what was required at any given moment, and could rise to any occasion. That earlier kiss, for example, was just a mechanical smoothing of her ruffled feathers before they embarked on their first social occasion together. And during the evening his behaviour towards her had shown exactly the right mixture of attentive solicitude and tender affection that would make any bride shine with happiness.

Any bride except herself! For she alone knew the value of his spurious charm. She had fallen victim to it once, hadn't she?

'Come along, darling,' he was saying, laughingly declining Piet's offer of 'one for the gravel drive.' 'I've got to make an early start tomorrow.' He turned back to their hosts. 'Thank you both. It's been a most enjoyable evening.'

Once they were out of the Sloots' sight Roz drew away from him. His touch had set her longing, and that could be almost lethal as far as she was concerned. His magnetism had seemed to grow each day, but she was determined not to succumb to it.

Back inside the house he said, smiling, 'Join me in a nightcap?'

'Is it obligatory?' The waspish riposte was out before she could stop it.

'No, just—companionable. Can't we try and make the best of things?'

She dredged up a great sigh. 'Oh, well—yes, I suppose we should.' Reluctantly she followed him into the big room. He turned on a lamp by the fire, instantly illuminating his strong, austere profile. She poured him a whisky and handed it to him as he sat down. Then, unaccountably nervous and edgy, she went over to the music centre, selecting a tape at random.

As the first strains of Schubert crept into the room he glanced up sharply, and Roz felt her face begin to burn. They had listened to this quintet together at a concert in York. Damn; better if she had chosen one of Ewan's Bix Beiderbecke numbers.

'At least we still have this in common—music,' said Nick, stretching out in his chair. 'And I liked your friends, too. It was a good evening. Incidentally, we shall be giving a few dinners ourselves. How's your cooking?'

The prosaic question dissipated the romantic nostalgia that the music had re-awakened in her. She looked at him, her eyes cool and challenging. 'Ewan tells me that I do a nice line in beefburgers and beans,' she answered.

He laughed. 'I was thinking along more elaborate lines,' he said.

'Have no fears, Nick. I won't shame you,' she said drily.

'I hadn't supposed for one moment that you would.' There was a small rebuke in his voice.

'Well, thank you for that vote of confidence, anyway.'

He was silent, and Roz began to feel her nervousness mount. Somehow there was an intimacy developing—perhaps the legacy of the pleasant evening they had spent together, and it could only threaten the control she had to impose upon herself in order to meet his. So she was relieved when he said, idly, 'Incidentally, a couple of days after I come back I have to attend a convention— at the Beauchamp Gorse Hotel on the south coast.'

'Oh? Isn't that the place for a great gastronomic experience? I think I read about it somewhere.'

'That's the place. So there's to be a big gathering of folks in the holiday business—and their wives.'

'I see.' Roz sat up straight, looking pleasantly alert. 'So this is one of the occasions you had in mind when you asked me to marry you?'

He gave a swift, savage frown, then just as quickly his brow cleared. 'That's right.'

'So what do I have to do?' she asked shortly. 'Not having had much experience of the high life, I must look to you for guidance.'

He refused to rise to the bait in her voice. 'Well, the members of the association attend seminars, hold discussions—that kind of thing. A Member of Parliament will no doubt take the platform. As for the wives—well, things are laid on for them. Usually a coach is booked to take parties to see the local sights. And then, of course, some of them play golf or bridge . . . go shopping. And in the evenings it's all very social.'

'It sounds fascinating,' said Roz doubtfully.

'Oh, you might even enjoy it if you really try. The point is,' he went on, putting down his glass and watching her carefully, 'you're going to need a couple of evening dresses at least. So go to York or Harrogate or Leeds or somewhere, and get yourself something really special. And,' he went on, a sudden frost sharpening his tone, 'I have to point out that these are not—how did you phrase it? Goodies and gifts? Or was it the other way round? As you suggested, those I will keep for—my other women. What I'm proposing is that you buy a—shall we say—working uniform? But make it glamorous.'

'But of course,' said Roz, her eyes disarmingly innocent. 'As I said before, I won't shame you.'

'Good. That's agreed, then.'

She winced at his hard tone and got up quickly. 'I'm going to bed,' she rapped out.

'Then goodnight. I won't disturb you in the morning. I'll probably be away before you're awake.'

'I wish you a pleasant journey,' she said as she went out. At least for the next couple of weeks she would have a respite from all the currents which Nick's presence stirred up, all the flashpoints which he touched off. There was a bleak kind of relief in the prospect.

CHAPTER SIX

Roz awoke the following morning, surprised that the feeling of elation she had anticipated was missing. Quickly she brushed her hair, her dark brows drawn in thought. This was the morning she had waited for, wasn't it? Nick would have gone; she would be her own woman again and could resume the work that she loved. And tonight Ewan would be home, and for two weeks things would be as they had once been before Nick came back into her life to make whirling dervishes of her emotions. But, despite these attempts at comfort, a faint sense of depression hung over her as she threw on a housecoat and went down to the kitchen.

Her heart sank as she saw Nick sitting at the big table, drinking black coffee and making notes on a small pocket-pad. He glanced up as she entered, then reached for the coffee-pot, drawing a cup and saucer towards him. 'Good morning, Rosamund,' he said politely. 'You'll have a cup?'

She shook her head. 'No, thanks. I really prefer tea in the mornings.'

He gave a slight inclination of his head. 'What a lot we don't know about each other,' he said. 'Yet once I felt that I knew you as I know myself.'

'That was a long time ago,' she answered with finality. She turned to fill the kettle and take milk from the fridge as he swallowed the last of his coffee, glanced at his watch, and rose, putting away his gold pen and notebook.

'The first thing I'll do when I get back is open a joint bank account—for the housekeeping and such,' he added pointedly. 'In the meanwhile I've left you a cheque on my dressing-chest, and for emergencies you'll find some cash in the top drawer. And,' he went on, his face breaking into an expression of slightly malicious amusement, 'I'm pleased to see that you're not smouldering at the mere mention of money.'

By comparison with the way Roz felt, Nick looked well-rested, alert and ready for whatever the day might bring. She caught the merest whiff of his subtle cologne—a scent that now seemed to have become part of every breath she took—and noticed the crisp handkerchief in the breast pocket of his suit, the brisk, sure movements of his hands as he checked the contents of his briefcase. He looked as if he could take on the world, she thought dully. 'And what are you going to do while I'm away?' He glanced up from beneath winging eyebrows.

'Get on with my work. Buy clothes as per your instructions, cook for Ewan and myself. And I'll go over and see your father sometimes,' she said carelessly, slotting bread into the toaster.

He gave her a friendly, impartial smile. 'Good. I'll call in myself. Even if he's still asleep, I'll be able to get a progress report from Nancy. Well, I'd better be off. Walk out to the car with me?'

'I could use a breath of fresh air,' she said, and saw by the sudden firming of his mouth that he had caught the asperity of her remark, although she hadn't meant it that way. Still, what did it matter?

There was a spangle of dew on the lawn, and from the old yew tree a thrush called repeatedly. Roz watched Nick stow his bag and briefcase in the car, then stood back as he opened the driver's door. 'I suppose I should wish you a successful trip,' she murmured.

'It's usual,' he agreed. 'And if anyone happened to be watching, then I'm sure they would attribute your look of subdued misery to the fact that you're broken-hearted to see me leave.'

'Then they couldn't be more wrong.'

'Spoken like the true new Roz I'm beginning to know,' he said lightly, glancing up. Then suddenly she was in his arms, his mouth stifling her protests, the iron of his muscles foiling her attempt to strain away from the warm, strong body.

Clad only in her thin nightdress and silky housecoat, Roz felt two islands of warmth on her back as his palms held her forcefully against him. His lips were cool and fresh and, in some indefinable way, reassuring. After a moment she closed her eyes, passively submitting her tired self to a momentary haven from the unhappy chaos of her thoughts. His warmth seemed to pervade her body, slowly and seductively. She sensed his power and the very essence which made him so different from the other men she had known. And despite herself her blood leapt.

Lingeringly he let her go. She looked up at him. Inexplicably she wanted to find some word that would begin to erase the bitterness that scummed their relationship. But, in view of the kind of man she knew him to be, it would be pointless. He lifted his wrist and glanced at his watch, then he raised both her hands to his face, laying his lips against each one in turn. She felt his breath whisper across her knuckles as he said, softly, 'Sorry about that little display, my dear, but it seems that our neighbours are early risers, too. Anna's at her bedroom window.'

Roz burned with an instant flare of bitterness. All the old feelings of rejection, humiliation and frustration welled up again inside her as, without knowing what she did, she reached out swiftly, her fingers filled with a sudden strength as they wound into his crisp hair. She pulled his face down towards her own, her mouth found his lips and, with a deliberation which seemed to come from a force outside herself, let the very tip of her tongue part them slightly. She felt his body suddenly clench and heard the ragged gasp he couldn't control. Then, still possessed by this perverse upsurge of strength, she put him away from her, her eyes shining with unshed tears.

'Strictly for Anna's benefit,' she explained bitterly. 'For we must promote the myth of a happy marriage, mustn't we? Well, how was that for a performance?'

'A *tour de force*, I'd say,' he breathed. 'Hell, you surely do choose your moments.'

She shook her head, her dark hair drifting across her face. 'No,' she said in a stricken voice, 'the moment chose me.'

It was only later, when she caught sight of the telephone-pad on the hall table, that she was reminded to ring Brad Williams. A pale smile flickered over her wide mouth as she wondered what Nick's reactions would be if he could see the lanky, jeans-clad youth whose message had prompted him to raise the point of men friends. Well, he need have no worries on that score, she thought derisively, for Brad was about twenty-three and had a live-in girlfriend, Becky, who was an artist.

Roz had first met Brad after an auction, when he had seen her struggling to get a chest into the back of her estate car and had come over to help. She saw him again a few weeks later at another saleroom and when, afterwards, she passed him loading his purchases into a battered blue van, she had stopped to say hello. 'How did it go?' she asked. 'Did you do any good here?' Then she had caught a glimpse of the broken furniture and boxes of miscellaneous metalware and had stopped, embarrassed.

Brad had interpreted her glance and grinned. 'Can't grumble. And, yes, I guess you'd call it the sweepings of the sty, but there's a good bit of old oak in there, and I've got a table at home that'll mend very nicely. Besides, someone's got to be down-market, you know.' He fumbled in his pocket and with a flourish produced a card. 'I'm a handy kind of bloke, so if you've any problems and think I can help, just give me a buzz.'

Since then Brad had twice done repair jobs which Roz couldn't handle, and had recently directed a customer her way. 'Dolls aren't my scene,' he had said, 'but I'm grateful for the commission.' He had tucked the notes away in a shabby wallet. 'What I need is a nice little job lot. I'm not out to make a million, just an honest living doing what I like to do.'

As Roz dialled his number, she reflected with affection that she and Brad understood each other perfectly.

His obvious pleasure when he heard her voice dispelled the lingering remnants of her early-morning gloom. 'But I understood you were away on honeymoon,' he exclaimed. 'Who's the lucky guy? Anyone I know?'

For a while they exchanged light-hearted banter, then Brad said, 'Am I glad to hear you! I've got an opportunity which might slip right through my fingers if I'm not quick. Listen, Roz, there's a chance for me to buy up the contents of an old outhouse. Tatty as hell—you know my line—but one or two pieces which, given the right treatment, will keep the wolf from the door. Trouble is—cash flow.'

'I get it,' Roz laughed. 'How much?'

'Four hundred. As soon as I've sorted the stuff out and toted some of it round to dealers, I know I'll be able to pay you back with interest. But it'll take a bit of time. And the trouble is, I've got a garage repair bill that won't wait.'

Roz thought furiously. She would like to help Brad, and, although she preferred to keep a reasonable amount of working capital in her bank account, there were no important sales coming up in the near future. And Nick had left enough money for day-to-day needs.

'All right. I'll let you have it,' she said.

'You're a doll,' Brad crowed. 'This is just the shot in the arm I've been needing. This afternoon, then?'

Roz replaced the receiver feeling happier than she had in weeks. Brad's call and her ability to help had put her on course again. Humming, she went over to the stables.

Ewan got home soon after seven, wrinkling his nose appreciatively as he came into the kitchen to find Roz basting a joint. 'What the——? I thought for a moment that I had come to the wrong house. You're supposed to be on honeymoon, aren't you? Don't tell me that Nick's walked out on you already!'

Roz closed the oven door and straightened up, turning to him with a face which she hoped expressed fulfilled love. 'Fool,' she laughed, then grimaced ruefully. 'Would you believe it, business interrupted? Nick's had to go to Bermuda. So it looks like I'm going to be a company widow. We came back yesterday.'

'Oh, that's grim,' Ewan sympathised. 'Well, I won't ask if you had a good time; one doesn't ask that kind of question. Anyway, I can see that you did.'

'No,' Roz murmured, 'one *doesn't* ask... And I wouldn't tell you if you did.' And if you knew the half of it, a quiet voice in her head added... But no, she had put a lid on that line of thought.

'I must say I missed your cooking,' Ewan said, going to the fridge and taking out a can of beer.

'Come to think of it,' Roz said, looking at him en-quiringly, 'you seem full of sweetness and light yourself.' Indeed, Ewan looked unusually smart, even brisk. In-stead of the porridgy shirts and mud-coloured ties he

wore with cords and tweed jacket, he was dressed in a
well-pressed suit over a striped shirt and toning tie. 'And
if you're surprised to find me here, then I was equally
surprised to find you *not* here. Where have you been,
or shouldn't I ask?'

'Ask away,' Ewan said sunnily, hanging his jacket over
a chair, 'for I've every intention of telling you.' He took
a long pull at his beer, then sat down, leaning his elbows
on the table. 'You're going to be even more surprised,
I think. It's quite a story.'

'Then I'm agog to hear it.'

'Well,' Ewan began thoughtfully, 'after the wedding
I came back here and the place seemed like a morgue.
I got to thinking...I saw just how I had moped
around——'

'No,' Roz put in gently, 'not moped: grieved. It was
understandable, Ewan.'

'But miserable for *you*.' He shot her a sympathetic
glance. 'And as if that wasn't bad enough, I'd been such
a bloody *fool*.' He raked his fingers distractedly through
his fair hair. 'No other word for it. And Nick—well,
that was an incredible stroke of luck, really—paid off
my debts. Roz, did *you*—well, I mean, did *you* have any
part in that?'

Roz concentrated on the mint she was chopping for
sauce. She had to be very careful here, for if Ewan
learned just *why* Nick had cleared his debts it would de-
molish him. 'Nick actually settled your——?' She turned
to stare at Ewan. 'Believe me, Ewan, *I* didn't persuade
him, if that's what you mean. The idea must have been
entirely his own.' That much, at least, was true. She
hoped that her surprised act was convincing.

'Oh, heavens,' Ewan said contritely, 'I hope I'm not
betraying any confidences. It was damned generous of
him to sort things out for me.'

Roz lifted the lid off a pan. 'Yes, it was,' she said after a moment. 'Still, didn't I tell you that he wouldn't stand aside and watch his own brother-in-law go under? He—I suppose he—lent you the money, then?'

'Lent? Nothing so lukewarm! And he didn't make a fuss about it, simply took me aside for a minute at the wedding reception and said that there was enough money in my account to take care of everything. It was a gift, he said, and the matter was closed. But I can't go along with that. I'm going to start paying him back just as soon as I can.' He set down his glass firmly, pushing back the lock of hair which had flopped forward. 'So now I'll tell you where I've been. To cut a long story short, I've been invited to join a panel of lecturers on printing-design. I'll still keep my little business going, of course, although I might have to delegate some... And once I've got a new system going at the office they'll be able to do without me for the odd couple of weeks when I'll be away.'

Roz heard his words as though from a distance. Her mind was still trying to assimilate the fact that Nick had *given* Ewan the money. Then why had he told her that it was a *loan*? She blinked rapidly; no time to think about the implications of that now, for Ewan was still talking.

'And it'll mean some trips abroad, of course, so I'm quite looking forward to it.'

'That's marvellous,' Roz said slowly. 'I—I'm surprised to hear about what Nick has done...' She stopped, biting her lip. 'Perhaps you *were* betraying a confidence,' she began, 'because Nick hadn't said anything to me about—giving you the money. So perhaps it would be as well if you didn't tell him that I know about the financial arrangements he made for you.'

'Oh, don't worry,' Ewan said with a laugh. 'It isn't a subject I care to raise, either with Nick or with you. I'm not proud of getting myself into such a jam. You know,

Roz,' he went on thoughtfully, 'he's a decent bloke. Once he had finished making me eat dirt—that night in April when he came here—he turned up trumps. I don't know what I would have done without...' He stood up. 'I'll go and change now. So, you see, this lecturing business will mean more money. More work, of course, and more hassle. But it's in a good cause. I'm going to surprise your old Nick with a cheque on the last day of each year.'

'Good for you,' Roz said heartily. And that, she thought triumphantly, is going to make Nick eat some of his words about Ewan.

With Ewan out of the room she could give her attention to what he had told her. So the money had been a gift, with no strings attached. That meant that she was free! There was nothing, now, to bind her to Nick. She could release herself from the trap which had enmeshed her since that cold April evening. Elation surged through her in a dizzying wave. And there was no need to ask herself exactly why Nick had insisted to her that the money was a loan which he would call in if she defaulted on their contract. No need at all. She could guess that it suited his egotistical nature to think that he had her exactly where he wanted her—subjugated, powerless, dancing to *his* tune. Oh, yes, she thought, stirring the gravy with unnecessary vigour, I see it clearly. As long as I believe that Ewan is in debt, albeit to Nick, then Nick thinks he holds all the cards. But I know different!

Briskly she dished up the vegetables. After this meal she could go up to Nick's room and pack his clothes, and when he came back she could tell him to go, that he had no hold over her whatsoever and that, by not telling her the truth, he had invalidated the contract as he had defined it.

It was a heady picture; she could now call his bluff and there wasn't a thing that he could do about it. This

would be *her* revenge! For hadn't he once made a fool
of her? Once that she *knew* about, she added bitterly.
And how many other times had there been—during a
love-affair which had meant the world to her—when he
had played a double game? Well, now she was in a position to turn the tables. And she would help Ewan to
repay the money. So, in the end, there would be no loss
of honour, of personal integrity.

The champagne feeling built up wildly. She imagined
Nick's face when he saw his suitcases standing in the
hall...

Then, in one stroke, her elation collapsed. She leaned
against the dresser, closing her eyes as all her energy
drained away. She wasn't free at all. Nick's gift put her
under a moral obligation that was far more restrictive
than a mere financial debt. And, in the final count, he
had given help when it was needed, saving her and Ewan
from a future which she had been unable to contem-
plate. Nothing could alter that. So, if anything, she was
even more deeply indebted to Nick for his monumental
generosity.

After supper she went upstairs. She felt restless, so it
would be no use going over to her workshop for she was
in no mood to concentrate on any one thing. Absently
she tidied her undies drawer, then drifted into Nick's
room. She tried to see it through his eyes. It did seem
meagre, she thought. And it must seem even more so to
him, used to the spaciousness of Meronthorpe and the
life-style he had enjoyed there. Although Grey Garth had
two other spare bedrooms, both much larger, this room
had been the only option because it adjoined her own.
So here she was, she reflected, back again to the business
of keeping up appearances.

She looked around vaguely. On the dressing-chest
stood a small bronze bust of the god Pan which he had
brought with him. The satyr face seemed to repel and

invite at the same time. She went over to it and traced
the curls, the pointed ears, with an idle finger, then her
glance fell on the little row of books that lay in a small
carved trough.

Slowly she picked one up. *The Collected Poems of
Louis MacNeice*. A tiny marker, the merest slip of paper,
protruded from between the pages. She opened it. A
stanza had been underlined, flooding her mind with
images of scent and shadow and a woman's curving hair.

Whose hair? she wondered, her heart twisting in
sudden pain. Which of the many women who had always
figured so prominently in Nick's life? Where was he now,
at this very moment? Above the earth, somewhere among
the stars? And was a woman with him? Or would that
happen in Bermuda?

She sank down on his bed, knowing the futility of
asking such questions of herself.

Grimly she drove herself during the next two weeks, ac-
complishing many of the jobs which she had postponed
during the weeks leading up to her marriage. Mentally
and physically she tried to exhaust herself so that she
would not think about him. There was plenty for her to
do, including four visits to Meronthorpe where Rolfe entertained her with old-world gallantry that, in other circumstances, would have made her feel wanted and
cherished by the Martel family.

She was still working after nine o'clock one hot
evening, engrossed in replacing the hair of a tiny wax-
headed doll. It was an eye-straining, exacting task, ne-
cessitating total concentration and deft fingers. Repeatedly Roz heated a tiny knife, cut small slits in the
wax and inserted a little tuft of hair, warming the wax
around it to melt slightly and hold the insertion.

After a while she straightened her aching shoulders,
blinking. Then her tired eyes opened wide as she focused

them on Nick leaning against the door, hands in pockets, chin sunk on chest, watching her with a steady, sombre gaze. She didn't know how long he had stood there, but instantly their eyes met her heart seemed to stop for a moment, then to thud in a heavy, torpid beat, slowly driving the blood into her pale face to drum against her temples.

'I would say you'd had enough,' Nick murmured, shouldering himself upright. 'Come along into the house now.'

'Ye-es.' Uncertainly she got up, putting the doll down gently and brushing the back of her hand across her hot forehead. 'I'm sorry—I had no idea that you would be home tonight.'

'How could you, when I didn't know myself?'

'You should have phoned from the airport.'

He tucked her arm into his as they went over the cobbles. 'I thought I'd give you a lovely surprise,' he quipped.

Roz felt weak. The strength she had drawn upon to exclude him from her thoughts during the past days was spent, yet with his fingers curved under her hand she needed it, now more than ever, to cope with the frissons that shivered up her spine. She drew away from him slightly. 'Or perhaps you thought you might surprise me in—in—what do they call it?'

'*Flagrante delicto?* Oh, Rosamund, what a nasty mind you have! And,' he added, laying a finger across her lips as she opened her mouth to speak, 'don't start getting uppity. I'm in no mood for it.'

She shot him a glare; with Ewan in the house, some pretence was called for, and this wasn't the moment to allow herself to be ruffled. All the same . . .

With his usual aplomb, Nick signposted the way for her. 'What a homecoming,' he said with mock-irritation as they went into the sitting-room where Ewan was halfheartedly watching a television play. 'Ewan, you've let my wife work herself to a standstill.'

'Huh, try and stop her when she's in that frame of mind,' Ewan grumbled comfortably from the depths of his chair. 'You'll learn, Nick.'

Roz looked brightly from one to the other. 'Would it be too much to ask that you don't talk about me as if I weren't here?' she laughed.

Nick looked at her critically, then put up his hand to brush her hair behind her ears, cupping her face in his hands. 'You've lost some weight, darling.'

'Just a little, I think.' Resolutely Roz smiled up at him.

'It must be love,' Ewan teased. 'It affects some women that way.'

'Oh, the voice of authority?' With relief, Roz looked across the room at her brother, stepping back from Nick's touch. 'I'll get you something to eat. You must be starving, Nick. Now, if only you had telephoned, then I would——'

'I stopped off for a snack. Just sit down, darling, and relax. Ewan, how about getting us all a drink? Lord, but I'm tired—nearly as tired as you, Rosamund.' He flashed her a disarming smile and reached for her hand, drawing her down on to the sofa beside him, then sliding his arm across her shoulders. After a second, she leaned against him, closing her eyes. But inwardly she felt that she was being stretched on a rack.

'Er—I'm just nipping out to the pub for an hour,' Ewan said, getting up, 'but I'll fix you a drink with pleasure before I go.'

Roz knew that he was trying to be tactful, and she couldn't tell which was worse—the charade she had to endure in his presence, or the prospect of being alone with Nick. She remembered their last moments together,

her unbelievable compulsion to kiss him wildly, and suddenly her face flamed.

As Ewan got the glasses and poured the drinks, she asked about Nick's trip, and spoke about his father, but as soon as Ewan left she got up abruptly. 'I hadn't realised just how exhausted I was,' she said. 'So I think I'll go up now.'

'I'll join you.' Nick stood up, draining his glass. 'After all, what's more natural for Ewan than to come in and find that we're both in bed? Two weeks is a long time for a newly married couple to be apart. And you certainly look as if you need your sleep. We mustn't have you exhausted *before* the convention, must we?'

She eyed him disparagingly. 'Anything you say, Nick,' she murmured meekly.

'Good. Perhaps we're getting somewhere at last. Good-night, Rosamund.' Outside her door he bent, brushing his lips against hers with a wing-like touch. Then he closed the door firmly behind him.

CHAPTER SEVEN

BEAUCHAMP GORSE was a converted country house built of honey-coloured stone and set in beautifully landscaped gardens. It had been adapted harmoniously, and little if any of its earlier graciousness had been lost in the transition to a more viable role.

Roz and Nick were shown to a large, sunny room whose elegantly swagged windows looked over a shrubbery ablaze with rhododendrons and azaleas. But her initial pleasure was completely eclipsed by the sight of the wide bed, and for a moment she recoiled. She turned to Nick, ready to protest, but the warning flash of his eyes stopped her. However, when the porter who had brought up their cases left, Roz flung round furiously. 'Not only a double bed,' she breathed in a stifled voice, 'but king-sized. You really do things in style, don't you?' Her eyes narrowed. 'What's the idea, Nick?'

He didn't answer but stood watching her, a lazy, mocking smile curling his lips, clearly enjoying her confusion.

'Oh, never mind,' Roz snapped. 'I don't want to hear.' She turned to go to the door.

'Where do you think you're going, Rosamund?' Nick said softly.

'Isn't it obvious? You don't seriously think I'm going to share a bed with you, do you? I'm going down to Reception to tell them that, in spite of Mr Martel's instructions, *Mrs* Martel would prefer two single rooms.'

He was beside her in one long stride, his grip hurting her wrist as he swung her round to face him. 'You'll do no such thing,' he said ominously.

Angrily she shook her arm free, her face white and set. 'Why not? It's a perfectly reasonable request. And one that *I* consider necessary. I must say, though,' she added, her voice icing over, 'I wouldn't have thought that even you would stoop to such a cheap trick. Did you expect I'd take it lying down?'

She saw a flicker of amusement break up his grim features, and realised her unfortunate choice of words. It made her angrier still that he could see *any* humour at all in the situation. 'Well, you can think again, Nick. My duties as a wife stop at a certain point. And I might remind you that when we—exchanged contracts, separate rooms were specified. That applied on our honeymoon, and at home. Naturally I thought it extended to—wherever we were. And now you have the——'

'Shut up,' he said sharply. 'Just stop ranting and listen, will you? In the first place, you don't have to spell out to me the conditions of our contract. I know them only too well. And in the second, it will surprise you, no doubt, to learn that I did not arrange this. All the reservations were made by the association's head office *en bloc*.'

Roz stared at him, uncertain whether or not to believe him.

'And in case you hadn't noticed, this must be one of the best rooms in the hotel——'

'As befits your exalted position, no doubt,' Roz sneered, trying to cover her chagrin with an edge of sarcasm.

'If you say so,' he retorted.

'Well, then, in that case the hotel will be only too anxious to pander to my whims and put the matter right, won't they?' She picked up her handbag from the peach bedspread where she had thrown it in her impatience. 'Unless, of course, you, as the man, would rather go down and ask for two——'

'Oh, for heaven's sake, don't be so damned stupid,' he ground out. 'You're becoming a bore, Rosamund, with your obsession that I'm panting to get you into bed against your will. What the hell do you think I am? You've had no complaints so far, have you? Any pointers in that direction have existed solely in your own mind. All I'm asking—and I'm surprised that I have to remind you yet again—is that we try to give the impression of a happily married couple. Surely that's not beyond your capabilities?'

'You make it more difficult all the time,' she whipped out, looking at him disgustedly. His eyes were as cold and hard as stones, his features unremitting in their severity.

'And if,' he continued, as if she hadn't spoken, 'that involves being *seen* to spend a night in the same room— which is perfectly normal for the said happily married couple—then so be it. Have you got that?'

'Do I have a choice?' she retorted.

'No,' he agreed, 'in the circumstances, you haven't. So for heaven's sake give in gracefully and stop rocking the boat at every turn. I have a heavy weekend ahead, and I can do without your fits of the vapours every few hours.'

'Fits of the vapours?' Roz's eyebrows rose almost to her hairline. 'Now you make me sound like some prim Victorian miss. And I suppose you see yourself as the dominant male whose orders make everyone jump to attention. That would seem to fit your role in this—this marriage,' she went on scornfully. 'Well, just get one thing——'

'Oh, shut up. For pete's sake, shut up! Must you persist in making things worse than they are?' He turned his back on her in a gesture of finality, opened his suitcase and began hanging away his clothes.

Seething and wordless, Roz watched him for a moment, then snatched up her sponge-bag. 'I'm going to have a shower,' she said curtly.

'Why not make it a real cold one? That might take some of the fire out of you.' He glanced up, his eyes bleak, his face set in lines of controlled exasperation.

With an exclamation of wordless anger, Roz closed the door firmly between them. In the luxurious bathroom she scrubbed her body pitilessly, as if to expunge the echoes of his scathing tones and the distaste in his face. She wondered desperately how long a marriage could last when such antagonism was so easily aroused. It couldn't be long now before Nick would finally accept that things weren't going to work out. And yet, she thought, rinsing off the fragrant lather, plenty of marriages based on similar foundations had eventually proved quite successful in the past, but that was probably because women had so small a say in matters. Things were different now, and she certainly wasn't the prim Victorian woman that Nick's words had suggested he wanted.

All the same, she thought disconsolately, reaching for the vast fluffy towel, she wished that she hadn't immediately jumped to the wrong conclusion about the reservation of their room; she had been hasty and now felt humiliated. This convention was important to Nick, and he had been perfectly logical in asking her not to rock the boat. She sighed deeply. Life would be decidedly more pleasant if she could manage to react less violently to him. Over-react, he had called it, in Venice. And perhaps he had a point, she conceded miserably. After all, where might she and Ewan be if Nick hadn't stepped in with this solution to their problems? Ewan's business would be on the way out, and right now they would be in the throes of selling Grey Garth, house-hunting on a low budget with the burden of debt hanging over them, inescapable and ever-present. So she had to admit—yet again—that she did owe Nick *some* consideration.

When she went back to their room Nick had stripped off his shirt and was bending over the chest of drawers, his back towards her. Her resolutely sensible evaluation of their relationship and the trite remark she had prepared to get them on to an even keel again dried up. She was aware of a sudden unevenness in her breathing. His tanned skin gleamed as if it were slightly oiled. As he moved she watched the play of reflected light ripple over his shoulders, catching his vertebrae. She felt a sudden scorching urge to run her fingertips over the polished skin. His muscles shifted, undulating the gleaming contours, and she glanced away quickly, frightened by her own erotic desire. Without a word he straightened and went into the bathroom as she began to unpack and put away her clothes.

She sank down on the dressing-table stool, clipping on garnet ear-rings with fingers strangely boneless and inexpert. Carefully she kept her eyes averted from the wide bed. At least it was big enough to allow plenty of space between them. But the chill of apprehension inside her persisted.

She stroked lip-pencil over her wide, mobile mouth, then automatically began to brush the straight dark bob. But the whole situation niggled like a sore tooth. Why was she making such a fuss? Nick was a very attractive man, and no one, least of all herself, could be blind to that. And just that one night with him had shown her the ecstasy of his loving. Both those factors were sufficient justification for some girls to want to go to bed with him without a second thought. But she wasn't *some girls*! She was *herself*—alternately loathing him and wanting him, and rarely able to strike the right note which would make this marriage bearable.

With reluctant feet she went over to the wardrobe and took out a dark crimson silk sheath and slipped it over her head, watching the soft, rich sheen settle over the mould of her slim figure. Then she added the matching velvet jacket embroidered with metallic thread and pearls. It was quite unlike anything she had ever expected to own, its design clearly influenced by the Tudor period, and she had been unable to resist it.

She hadn't heard Nick come back into the room, but beyond her reflection in the mirror she suddenly saw his face, his expression blank and indifferent.

'Like it?' she asked, her mouth dry. 'I'm afraid it was terribly expensive,' she added tentatively.

'But worth every penny,' he said in a strangled voice.

So he was still angry with her, she thought, her heart sinking. 'So I won't—won't let you down?'

'On the contrary, you'll do me proud,' he said shortly.

Nervously she took his arm as they reached the bottom of the stairs and went into the large salon which had been reserved for the welcome cocktail party. Masses of flowers grouped on gilt console tables were duplicated in the tall pier glasses behind. The elaborately coffered ceiling looked freshly painted, white and pale green and gold. The chandeliers glittered like drops of living water above waiters moving serenely with trays of drinks among the groups of people already gathered.

A slight hush seemed to fall upon the room as Roz and Nick went in. Shrewdly she realised that there might have been a certain amount of speculation about the girl whom Nick had chosen to marry, and she was suddenly aware of a crippling lack of confidence.

Nick's arm pressed lightly against her side. 'You've made quite an entrance, I'd guess,' he murmured. 'So relax. You have absolutely nothing to fear.'

How had he managed to read her thoughts? Roz wondered, but the question was fleeting as they were quickly
absorbed into a group of middle-aged men and their
wives. Roz felt herself to be under scrutiny, but hid her
nervousness with a pleasant smile which equally parried
the admiration in the men's faces and the speculation
behind the women's glances.

'Well, well,' said a bluff white-haired man who had
been introduced as Vic, 'we wondered when Nick would
finally weaken. Now we know what he was waiting for!'

Roz's shy dimple came as she murmured her thanks,
and for a few minutes they all chatted generally, men-
tioning names unfamiliar to Roz, and then she was drawn
into the women's talk. She was very conscious of Nick,
never far from her, and she noticed the respect he commanded among these affluent, worldly people. This rich
room and its glittering company seemed a world away
from her smelly stable workshop and the green spaciousness of the Dales. Yet Nick seemed able to adapt
to both with the ease of a chameleon, she thought.

She was aware of one of the women eyeing her dress
thoughtfully, with admiration. 'Trust Nick,' the woman
said warmly, but somehow the implied compliment did
not quite disguise a certain waspishness in her words.

Roz raised an ingenuous eyebrow. 'I'm sorry?' she
murmured.

The woman smiled. 'Well, one wouldn't expect Nick
to marry the stereotyped little *ordinary* country mouse.'

'Oh, I don't know,' Roz demurred softly. 'Even mice
have their fanciers, I believe.'

A rather gaunt woman, Margaret, whose expensive
dress didn't look quite right on her, laughed. 'That's one
for *you*, Eve,' she said. Turning to Roz with a smile that
softened and beautified her face, she explained, 'I'm a
country girl myself. Mind, I *look* it.' She laughed again.
'Nowhere like it, I always say. Confidentially, I loathe

these ritzy get-togethers, but needs must when the devil drives, and Arthur can be quite a devil at times. Still, at least there's the consolation of some good golf quite close. Do you play, my dear?'

'I'm afraid not,' Roz smiled.

'Bridge, then?'

Roz shook her head, suddenly finding the confidence to be frank. 'Neither of them has ever appealed to me,' she said, 'so I've never bothered to learn.'

'Nor does she have the time,' Nick said suddenly at her elbow. Roz felt his arm go around her waist. 'My wife has a thriving business.'

'Oh, so you married a career woman?' Eve smiled archly up at Nick.

'Antique restoration,' he said succinctly. 'Dolls and other collector's items,' he went on, with a fond smile for Roz.

One of the women, Polly, who had remained quiet, turned an interested face to Roz. 'That sounds fascinating. My son collects automata...' Within a few minutes Roz was talking authoritatively and animatedly, grateful for Nick's interjection which seemed to raise her status here, before he had turned back to the men.

'So, with a business of your own,' Eve said, 'you won't be jetting around the world with Nick on his travels?'

'Oh, sometimes I will,' Roz said airily, 'but, as you say, with a business...'

'Well, I don't think *I'd* want to let him loose,' Eve remarked, with an assessing glance at Nick's back.

Nick had caught her words, and he turned suddenly, smiling creamily. 'But my wife trusts me,' he said softly.

Roz couldn't meet his eyes. She looked down at her glass, then took a sip of her drink.

'Isn't that right, darling?' Nick pursued, in the same velvet tones.

She returned his gaze with a frank expression. 'But of course,' she exclaimed. And despite herself her mouth curved in a smile. What a crazy game this was! Then she gathered from Nick's approving inclination of his head that she was playing it to the right ground rules.

All the while they were chatting more people were arriving in groups and couples. Then suddenly Roz glanced towards the doorway and for a moment her gaze was held. A girl had come in, unaccompanied. Tall and willowy, she was clad in a simple black dress whose lines betrayed its couturier label. She wore her silver-blonde hair taken severely off her face into a smooth chignon. For a moment she was quite still, a half-smile warming her expression, then a group near the door saw her and drew her into their midst.

'Ah,' Polly said, 'I see Gabriella is here. I wondered if she would be. Well, at least that should please...some of the men,' she finished lamely. She took a quick drink, and suddenly Roz was aware of the hesitation in her remark and the confusion that followed. Aware, too, that a tiny silence had fallen over the women she was with.

Her skin seemed to prickle as it picked up possible signals. What had Polly been about to say? What might she have said if she hadn't suddenly remembered that— that Roz was beside her? Could it be that Gabriella's appearance might have pleased...Nick?

A sudden flush of heat ran through Roz, so that she wanted to throw off the velvet jacket. Now why on earth should she think that? It was a crazy thought, almost paranoid. And yet... Trying to find justification, she looked around. Most of the people here were middle-aged, some even elderly. And, without doubt, the two most charismatic people present were this—Gabriella and Nick.

'Have you ever met Gabriella?' Eve was asking. Roz snapped her attention back, aware of a shrewd watchfulness in the pale blue eyes.

'No, I haven't. She's very lovely,' Roz said politely.

'Who are you talking about?' Margaret turned away from the small, plump woman she had been speaking to. 'Oh, I see. Mrs Gabriella Paget. Yes, she *is* lovely. I think we should all watch our menfolk when she's around. Now, my dear,' she added hastily, patting Roz's hand, 'I don't mean that unkindly. I hardly know the girl, but she seems a sweet creature. But she certainly has a knack of bringing out the chivalry in the men. Even the chairman—and confidentially he's a crusty old soul—even *he* was running around offering her his umbrella last year and being generally protective and solicitous.'

'I can't see why he should,' Eve said spikily. 'Gabriella's not the fragile kind. She's done very well for herself. You must meet her, Roz. She's around your age, I'd say, or a couple of years older.'

'Oh, you'll meet her,' Margaret said vaguely. 'She's a great friend of Nick's. You'll like her.'

Roz felt her smile tighten like a face mask. Obviously Margaret's remark was innocent. But there was something in Eve's eyes, and in Polly's silence, after that first embarrassed remark, that seemed to hold a significance for her. What were they suggesting?

Angry with herself, she slammed a shutter down on such questions. It was completely irrational that the mere sight of the tall, svelte figure, now talking animatedly to the group she was with, should spark off such a feeling of sickening isolation in her. She glanced at Nick, but he was in earnest conversation with a large, bearded man and appeared not to have noticed Gabriella's entrance. But surely that, in itself, was suspicious; who could have failed to see the elegant woman who had paused—deliberately?—in the doorway and who, even now as one of the crowd, seemed to stand out from the rest? Might not Nick's apparent ignorance of Gabriella's arrival be—deliberate? I'm going crazy, she told herself. And then—no, I'm not; I *know* Nick.

There was a rustle of movement through the room. Nick was by her side. 'Dinner,' he said, then he caught sight of Gabriella and waved.

It wasn't until after the long, leisurely meal and the welcoming speech that Roz met her. At close quarters she saw that Gabriella's skin was flawless, and that her eyes matched the long jade ear-rings that swung against her slender neck—the only jewellery she wore apart from her wedding ring. As Nick introduced them Roz had a strange, niggling conviction that they had already met, but this was quickly explained when Nick referred to an article, with photograph, which had been published about Gabriella in a national newspaper supplement.

Roz wondered where Gabriella's husband was. Clearly she was here alone, so perhaps he was abroad... What had Eve said? Something about Gabriella having done very well for herself? She certainly looked the product of a very privileged life-style, Roz decided.

'Gabriella runs an outfit for single parents,' Nick explained. 'And from what I gather, it's going very well.'

Gabriella smiled. 'Now, Nick, Rosamund must be feeling absolutely saturated with the holiday scene,' she protested, 'and I'm sure she doesn't want to hear about One Plus—that's the name of my company,' she added, turning to Roz.

'Oh, I'd love to hear about it,' said Roz politely.

'You're just being kind.' Gabriella's green eyes wrinkled attractively as she laughed. 'But actually I don't seem able to talk of much else these days, so I'll tell you, anyway. When I see you yawn, I'll stop.'

She paused for a moment, then said, 'Generally, when you think of an activity holiday, or a cultural or educational one, you imagine retired couples, or people without children, or a few loners painting away or listening to music or—or whatever. But my contention is that there must be thousands of one-parent families with children who would love to join in some activity, but end up at the seaside because of the kids. So I provide the complete package. Mum and Dad pack up their paints or go off on an archaeological dig, while activities are arranged for the children. That way everyone's happy; the parent doesn't feel cramped or frustrated, and the children don't have to be parked with grandparents.'

'And it's working all right?' Nick looked at her. The green eyes were almost on a level with his own, Roz noticed.

'It's working. Thanks to you, Nick darling.'

'Oh, come on. I only pushed the idea along a bit——'

'But you put me on to that super place in the Lakes, and if you hadn't had a word with——'

'Enough!' Nick laughed. 'What are friends for?' He turned to Roz. 'Another drink, darling?'

When he had gone to the bar, Gabriella said, 'I love your jacket; it's perfect—on you.'

'Thank you.' Roz felt stiff and unresponsive, although so far as she could see Gabriella was, indeed, a 'sweet creature.'

'I had wondered what Nick's wife would be like,' Gabriella was saying. 'I hope you'll both be very happy.'

'Thank you,' Roz said again.

'He's really something special, isn't he?'

'Well, naturally, *I* think so.' Roz wished that Nick would come back. She groped for something to say, and eventually came up with, 'We had a very quiet wedding, otherwise no doubt Nick would have sent you an invitation. I gather that you're old friends. Have you any children?'

'No.' Gabriella's green eyes clouded for a moment, and Roz regretted her question. 'But I love children, and that's why I'm so enthusiastic about One Plus.'

'Yes, I can understand that. It seems a very worthwhile job. Ah, here's Nick.'

Soon they were joined by Vic and the bearded man, and Roz was relieved when the conversation became general again. Surreptitiously she glanced at the gilded sunburst clock on the wall above the door, and with a sense of impending doom saw that it was slightly after midnight. Already people were beginning to drift away. The thought of the night ahead filled her with a cold dread, and she knew that the veneer of dignity which she had tried to sustain would be severely threatened by the situation where she and Nick slept together yet maintained the distance which had been dictated by the terms of their marriage. As Nick glanced at his watch, raised his eyebrows questioningly towards her, murmuring that he had a long day ahead and that they ought to think of going, she had to control a sweeping sense of panic.

She undressed quickly in the bathroom, and when she went into the bedroom again she saw that Nick was already in black silk pyjamas. He didn't speak, and when he came back from the bathroom Roz was lying on her side at the very edge of the bed. 'Goodnight, my dear,' Nick said with a throb of amusement in his deep voice. Then he turned out the light.

Roz knew that she would never sleep. The events of a crowded day flickered across her mind like a speeded-up film. Every cell of her body cried out its awareness of Nick, so close and yet so far away. She thought that she could feel the warmth of his body, hear his breathing;

even her flesh seemed to tingle as if he were touching her on her hips, her thighs... How long could she go on like this? It was unbearable... She willed herself to relax, muscle by muscle, until at last sleep came, and with it the dream she dreaded. She had had this same dream several times after her mother's death and twice before her marriage.

The beach was the same; the shelving wet shingle sucked at her toes as she tried to run away from the incoming tide and that one monumental wave that curled over her like the open maw of a voracious beast. And the colours were always the same; in the curl of water towering almost above her head she saw the streaks of citrus yellow, the purple, the lurid magenta, the luminous, terrifying red. And there was the noise, the ear-filling roar rising to a climax as the wave broke in a storm of spray and she tried to scramble up the steep incline, slithering and stumbling over the sucking, treacherous shingle. The water receded and she shook with relief. But only for a moment, for the wave gathered again, sucking up water and sweeping towards her to crush and drown... She heard her own whimper, felt her body drenched and cold as her feet sought purchase in the unstable ground...

Then a voice was saying, 'Wake up. It's all *right*... You're here. Safe. Hush now, everything's all right.'

Weeping with a mixture of fright and relief, she turned blindly in Nick's arms. Her heart was still pounding, gripped by the echo of her terror, and her body was chilled and wet, not with spray but with her own drenching fear... She wiped her eyes against the warm silk of his shoulder and let her breath go out in a shuddering sob. 'Oh,' she whispered faintly, 'it was—a dream. I've had it before. Even while I'm dreaming I remember the other times... It's...' A tremor shook her again, and the arms around her tightened.

'Stop thinking about it,' he commanded gently. 'It's over. Just lie quietly for a while.'

Gradually her heartbeat slowed, and her breathing grew more regular. But the horror of that cold, brown beach and the roaring anger of the wave had drained her. Her limbs felt heavy and immovable.

Nick brushed the damp hair from her forehead and she began to relax against him, moving her head slightly to lie gratefully on his chest. She heard the harsh intake of his breath and knew that she must move, right away, into the privacy of her own edge of the bed. But her body felt almost anaesthetised.

He was still soothing her, his hands moving gently over her bare shoulders. She couldn't hear him breathing, and she wondered idly if he was holding his breath. The room was so still, so warm and safe and dark... Then her breath quickened, and she made an attempt to move away from him. But the motion brushed her breast against his hand, and instantly his arms were iron bands crushing her against him. She lifted her face and his mouth came down upon her lips in a kiss of unfathomed intensity. The narcosis of the dream's aftermath vanished. She put out her arms to hold his shoulders closely against herself, her lips parting in a sigh of pleasure, opening to the probe of his tongue, and she felt herself lit by the sweet beginnings of passion. His hands moved over her hips, his fingers spread, and down to her thighs, then began to stroke slowly upwards so that her nightdress was coaxed higher, baring her skin to his touch. His lips still holding her prisoner he raised his chest above her as he drew up the lacy covering. In the darkness she saw the pale blur as he threw it over his shoulder.

Her arms wound around his neck, drawing him down again, turning her head on the pillow so that his lips were against her ear, his breath uncoiling delicious desires inside her. Then he began to drop tiny, impatient kisses like rain, from her hairline, over her nose, her lips, chin, throat, until they reached the dark valley between her breasts. She moved voluptuously, and a ragged gasp tore through him as his hands slid over her hot, moist skin to cup her breasts for a moment, his forefinger feathering light circles around her stiffening nipples.

The room seemed to spin away as sensation mounted inside her like an ascending rocket. She writhed in his arms, and with hands suddenly rough with pent-up longing she tore off the silk jacket that separated their flesh. The dampness of her body slid against his skin, absorbing his heat, answering his potency with her own exquisite arousal.

They moved together, limbs entwined, thigh caressing thigh, hands finding sensual bliss, lips tasting skin, their breath mingling in impatient unison. *This,* she thought disjointedly... *This* is why there can never be anyone else... She gave a broken moan, and he slid her body under his and she buried her face in the dark hollow of his neck. 'You're mine,' he said harshly against her hair. 'You belong with me, and don't ever forget it, darling.'

She felt his hands under her hips, raising her towards him. Then they were one body, driven by a rhythm older than man as they moved towards the complete fusion of all the pleasure the body was capable of giving. The heat inside her seemed to burst, her limbs to melt as their shared compulsion whipped the tempo to a frenzy, and Roz's gasp of elation was lost in Nick's cry of release.

For a while they lay together, spent and at peace. There seemed no need for words. Together they had performed an act of love, and to Roz this was a commitment deeper than the marriage service. Satiated, safe and deliriously happy, Roz didn't want to talk now. The words could come tomorrow. Simply by finding each other and learning each other as they had tonight, the experience was complete in itself.

'What *was* the dream?' Nick whispered, his lips nibbling the skin of her shoulder.

'The——? Oh, I'd forgotten about that ... There was a terrifying, gigantic wave about to break over me...' she murmured drowsily.

His breath warmed her as he laughed quietly. 'They do say,' he said softly, 'that dreams of water have sexual connotations.'

'Do they? Then perhaps they're right.' She stretched luxuriously. 'Perhaps...' But she didn't finish the sentence. Sleep, sound and undisturbed, closed her heavy eyelids.

CHAPTER EIGHT

WHEN Roz awoke Nick was gone. Her watch showed twenty minutes past nine. For a while she lay masochistically enjoying the pleasurable soreness of her body. Her lips felt swollen and ripe, the skin of her breasts was slightly pink. A fugitive, secret smile widened her mouth for a moment as she relived his touch, his storming passion, the utter authority of his body. And now, at last, they would be able to talk. She could tell him of her feelings of two years ago, of the insecurity she felt in loving a man like him. Yes, they both had to talk; there were questions and answers. Afterwards perhaps they could go to Venice again. And this time it would be gloriously free from the constraints of their honeymoon.

She lay for a while savouring a future that, at this time yesterday, would have seemed impossible. Then quickly she got out of bed, picked up the telephone and ordered breakfast.

While she waited she bathed and dressed, still thinking of Nick, wondering if he were thinking of her. She knew that this morning someone or other was presenting a paper on insurance. It sounded horribly boring, she thought with a grin. They would have a short break for coffee at eleven.

Already little *frissons* of anticipation at seeing him again stirred inside her. She would look at his face and know, immediately, how he felt. Would last night's lovemaking still glow in his eyes as it did in hers? Had he, too, recognised that the old magic closeness was back?

One glance at him would tell her, confirm what she instinctively felt to be true.

She finished her toast and saw that there was still an hour to go before he would be free. It seemed like an age. She tidied the room, did her nails again, then changed from the lilac and white knitted suit she had selected earlier into a cream linen dress with an importantly buckled belt, and clipped on toffee-coloured amber ear-rings. And still there were twenty-five minutes to go. Excited and restless, she walked around the room, wandered into the bathroom, unscrewed the top of his after-shave and sniffed intoxicatingly, closing her eyes and trying to recreate his presence. Heavens, she thought, I'm like a teenager, wild with first love.

But why wait here? Why defer the moment of seeing him? She could go down and linger in the hall until he came out of the meeting. She would watch his face as he caught sight of her...

As she picked up her handbag from the dressing-table, her reflection seemed bright with an inner light, her mouth curved happily, and her dark eyes were pansy-soft and inviting. Her step was light as she almost danced out of the room and down the broad, shallow staircase.

She passed one of the small lounges where an earnest bridge party was in progress. None of the players saw her pass. She grimaced and moved on. Beyond the wide portico she saw Eve and three other women stowing golf-clubs into the boot of a car drawn up on the sweep of gravel. She paused for a moment under the portrait of some long-gone Beauchamp woman dressed in the fashion of the Restoration period.

Then, from a corridor that ran off to the left of the rear entrance she heard a door open and the hum of voices. So the meeting was over, and in a moment Nick would come round the corner. *Please*, she prayed, please let him make for our room, hurrying as if he can't wait to see me. Then let him catch sight of me. And then I'll know... She stood in the recess, her heart in her eyes.

Then she gasped, stunned. There was Nick, all right, but he wasn't alone. Gabriella was with him. But this morning she looked quite different. Her hair fell in a smooth, pale bell on to her shoulders. And in the fleeting moment it took for them to reach the french doors, Nick's arm slid across Gabriella's shoulders, and her blonde head tipped slightly towards him in the gesture which had been etched on Roz's memory one rainy February evening just over two years ago. But on that occasion Nick and Gabriella had been sitting in a car, dimly obscured by a rainswept window; *now* they were going out of the hotel, almost running into the sunshine as if they couldn't wait to be alone.

Dazed, Roz found herself going back up the stairs, crouching slightly as if to protect and cradle the enormous hurt where her stomach should be.

It seemed a long way back to the room which she had left, radiant with happiness, only a few minutes ago, and by the time she closed the door behind her the anaesthesia of shock was beginning to wear off. So those slight suspicions which had crept in during the cocktail party—prompted by Polly's embarrassment and the watchful speculation in Eve's eyes—*were* justified, after all. Gabriella. After two years, Gabriella was still in Nick's life.

Roz sank down on the bed, staring dully ahead, oblivious of everything except the questions hammering in her brain. Why, for heaven's sake, had Nick bothered to marry her when Gabriella was obviously of long-standing importance to him? But then, she reminded herself, Gabriella was already married. Hadn't Eve remarked that Gabriella had done well for herself? Roz closed her eyes against the pain which seemed to permeate every nerve of her limp body. Perhaps Gabriella was unprepared to give up the life she led, while accepting the heaven-sent opportunity of gatherings such as this, when she and Nick could get together with impunity.

Roz felt a wintry desolation settle over her. She went into the bathroom and got a glass of cold water, drinking it so quickly that its iciness ached in her forehead. But she couldn't stop thinking, turning things over... Nick had helped Gabriella to secure a holiday property in the Lake District... That, also, must have provided a watertight excuse for them.

So where do I fit in? Roz asked herself numbly. As a front? Was that what Nick had had in mind when he proposed? A protective camouflage to shield himself and Gabriella from wagging tongues?

People—like Polly and Eve—might speculate about Nick and Gabriella; they would wonder and concede that it was possible; then they would probably dismiss it as unlikely in view of Nick's recent—and apparently happy—marriage. And Gabriella's reputation would be protected.

With a dazed shake of her head, as if to free it from the thoughts that swarmed like hornets in her brain, she picked up the telephone and briskly asked the receptionist to order her a taxi straight away. It didn't take more than a moment to pack her sponge-bag and jewellery and the nightdress which Nick had drawn off with such urgency ten hours ago. Making a tight ball of it she stuffed it into her small case and closed it. From the wardrobe she took down the jacket that matched her linen dress. Beside it hung the dress she had bought for the grand farewell ball to be held tomorrow night: smooth, gleaming slipper-satin, shading from the palest eau-de-Nil to a deep indigo, cut on the bias so that it clung to her body to a point just above the knee at the back, where it flounced into a fishtail, sparkling with sea-coloured glittering beads. A mermaid dress, she had thought when she first saw it ... She winced, leaning her head against the open wardrobe door for a moment. The sea ... That had been the cause of it ... The wave, and the dream. And Nick's arms around her, meaning *nothing*.

She strangled a sob as she crossed to the writing-table and took from the stationery rack a sheet of the hotel's thick, embossed notepaper. 'I've gone home,' she wrote. 'I've had enough.' With hands resolutely steady and strong, she folded the paper, slipped it into an envelope and propped it against the bedside-lamp. Then she picked up her case and went down.

Let me get away before Nick comes back in, she prayed silently. If he has to see me, then let it be in the foyer, because there, short of making a scene and physically restraining me, there will be nothing he can do to stop me going. That is, she added cynically, if he *wants* to stop me. And why should he, with Gabriella here? I've served my purpose, established the image of a happily married man. He will probably invent some facile explanation for my departure—tell them all that I was called away to a sick relative or something. He is good at lying, both in the word and in the deed.

When the taxi dropped her off at Brighton station the London train was in, and during the short journey Roz kept her eyes fixed on the countryside beyond the window, determinedly blanking out all thoughts of Nick.

On the connection travelling north she politely discouraged the man sitting opposite who showed an inclination to talk and opened the magazine she had bought and pretended to read. The agony inside was steadily being replaced by an iron self-control. She tried to view the events of the past twenty-four hours rationally, firmly closing her mind to the emotional issues and concentrating purely on the practical side. Viewed flatly from this angle, her sudden departure from the hotel seemed a trifle melodramatic; after all, it had never been part of the agreement that Nick should change his ways. So why should the sight of him with Gabriella have had such a shocking, shattering impact? He was simply running true to form, wasn't he?

It was fortunate that Ewan had gone up to Edinburgh and so would not witness her premature return alone. But she wasn't looking forward to being on her own at Grey Garth with no diversion to take her mind off her troubles.

She unlocked the door to the shrill of the hall telephone. Her heart plummeted; she wasn't up to dealing with Nick's rage yet. She didn't want to hear his voice, let alone his opinion of her action.

Slowly she picked up the receiver, then went weak with relief when she heard Brad Williams' voice. 'I've been trying to reach you all day,' he complained, 'so I'm glad to have caught you now. Doing anything tomorrow?'

'Why...no. Nothing special, that is,' she said, recovering quickly. 'Why do you ask?'

'I've got a client for you. One good turn deserves another. Listen, Roz, I've got to go out, so I'll make it quick. This bloke—name of Coran Rivers—is setting up a childhood museum. I met him at... Oh, never mind all that, it's a long story. Anyway, I told him a bit about you and he's distinctly interested. Money no object, I gather. The thing is, can you see him tomorrow? He's doing a fair amount of travelling around and moves on again on Sunday.'

'Well—yes, all right. Shall I get in touch with him? Have you got his telephone number?'

'Oh, leave that to me. I have to call him about some other business anyway. So I'll tell him to come and see you—when? Around three o'clock?'

'Fine. Thank you, Brad.' She replaced the receiver and went into the kitchen to poach an egg. After she had eaten, she changed into slacks and shirt and went over to the stables. A few finishing touches were needed on two dolls, and there were minute curtains to be hung in the doll's house. The place could do with a thorough tidying, too, if she were to show her stock tomorrow. Willingly she set to work, glad to fill the hours which seemed so bleak and lonely a prospect.

She hadn't known quite what to expect in Coran Rivers. At first sight he was older than she had anticipated: his hair, although thick and beautifully groomed, was silver, and his figure more august than youthful. But when he smiled he shed the years, and a certain eager spontaneity in his movements made her revise her opinion.

After he had introduced himself she took him over to the stable, where he showed a keen interest in her stock. 'I do hope you're well insured,' he murmured, lifting the hair of a doll to look at the maker's mark, and grimacing with approval.

'Oh, yes,' Nick had updated her insurance immediately they came back from Venice. But she mustn't think of Nick now. She concentrated hard on Coran Rivers' hands—big and capable and looking rather incongruous as he picked up a doll and lightly touched the swansdown trimming of the tiny muff. 'Brad told me that you were hoping to open a children's museum.'

'Yes.' He laid the doll in its tissue-lined box. 'It's by way of being a memorial—to my wife.'

'Oh, I'm sorry... I mean, I didn't——'

'Know? No, of course you didn't.' He smiled. 'May I call you Roz? Anne died a year ago. She loved children. We had only one daughter, unfortunately, and she was drowned in a boating accident when she was seventeen.'

Roz looked at him, her eyes soft and sympathetic. What could she say to this big, bluff man who had known so much tragedy?

'I usually have tea at this time,' she ventured tentatively. 'Will you join me, Mr Rivers?'

'Coran, please.' His blue eyes twinkled. 'I'd be delighted. I think I've seen all I need to see. Obviously you love your work.'

'Yes, but then one must, otherwise it would seem so— so mediocre,' she added with a little laugh. 'The trouble is that often I hate parting with some of my stock. Fortunately I know that most of it goes to good homes where it will be treasured and cared for. These dolls are not for playing with. I often marvel that they've survived for so long. I guess Victorian children must have been more careful than today's kids.'

'Well, the Victorians had a very healthy—some might say unhealthy—respect for property.'

Roz laughed. She found that she could talk easily to him, and over tea in the garden she relaxed completely. She couldn't help feeling a glow when he listened to her so appreciatively as she talked about her work, and an anecdote about her snipping tiny locks off her own hair to cover the head of a bald doll had him laughing heartily. At last she stood up, picking up the tea-tray. 'I didn't realise the time,' she said. 'It's——'

'Almost half-past six. And I've kept you from other things,' he added.

'No, not at all. I've enjoyed our afternoon. But I seem to have done most of the talking, and I haven't heard anything about your plans for a museum.'

He sat back, smiling. 'We could talk about that over dinner, if you're agreeable. But perhaps you have other arrangements?'

She hesitated for a moment, then said, 'No, it's a lovely idea. I'm longing to know where some of my dolls will find a resting place—that is, if any of them are suitable.'

'Oh, yes. And the doll's house, and one or two of the other toys. Where shall we go? I don't know the area well.'

'I think—Lombards'. I must change first, though.'

Over the meal he talked a little about his wife and the work she had done with children, and of the children who had come to stay with them from time to time.

'Well, I think your idea of a memorial to so much happiness is perfect. Where will the museum be?'

'That has yet to be decided,' he answered. 'An industrial town, I think. I have a few avenues to explore yet. And of course there's the Trust to be set up and a great deal of work for me to do.'

'Which I'm sure you'll relish,' Roz remarked, swirling the brandy in her glass.

'Yes.' He nodded. 'I will. I've done very little this past year, I'm afraid.' He glanced at his watch and beckoned for the bill.

As he opened the car door for her outside Grey Garth, Roz said politely, 'Will you come in? For a last drink?'

'Thank you,' he said gravely. 'Just a quick one. I've got quite an area to cover tomorrow.'

The summer evening had clouded over and a storm was gathering, dimming the long, cool sitting-room with blue shadows as Coran and Roz went in. She turned on the lamps and poured him a drink as lightning flickered vaguely over the distant hills.

His company today had successfully occupied Roz's mind, but now, back at home, she quailed inwardly at the thought of the furore which she knew Nick would unleash when he returned the following day. Although she had felt a certain relief that he hadn't found it necessary to telephone her, now she almost wished that he had; at least that might have blunted the initial edge of his rage. And now tomorrow was almost here... The reckoning...

But none of her apprehension showed as she passed Coran a brandy which he took smilingly, raising the glass to her. 'Here's to my venture,' he murmured. 'You know, Roz, you're a nice person to be with—restful, relaxing.'

If you only knew how I felt inside at this very minute, she thought wryly. But she smiled back at him. 'You make me sound like an old sofa.'

'Far from it, my dear. It was meant as a compliment.'

'Yes, I know, Coran. And thank you.'

'I've enjoyed the evening so much. It's a long time since I've had such an attractive dinner date.' The lines deepened around the blue eyes. 'Oh, I don't mean merely physically attractive, but—our conversation, the whole ambience. Suddenly life doesn't seem such a dull burden, after all. If I'm honest, I have to say that since Anne died I've indulged my self-pity. But now that this museum project seems to be gathering momentum things look altogether brighter all round.'

'Of course they do,' she said warmly. 'You've begun to look outwards again, and it's a challenge.' She stood up. 'Another brandy?'

'Better not. I'm driving, remember? Oh, there was one thing that I thought you might——' He stopped suddenly, arrested by the swish of tyres over the gravel outside.

Swallowing an icy lump which had gathered spontaneously in her throat, Roz turned quickly towards the window as Nick's headlights swept past, lighting a momentary reflection in the mirror hanging on the opposite wall.

'Your husband?' Coran asked.

She nodded brightly, glueing a smile on her stiff lips. 'I wasn't expecting him until tomorrow.' She cleared her throat and nervously smoothed her hair, a gesture which didn't escape Coran.

'You seem a little—uneasy. Shouldn't I be here? I mean, surely he wouldn't——'

'Heavens, no!' Roz exclaimed, too quickly. 'He knows that I have business contacts, naturally. And as I do business from home, then it's obvious that sometimes...' Her voice died. She felt that she was being too vehement, so she went on more calmly, 'I'd like you to meet him. I think that——'

She broke off as Nick opened the door. Roz realised that the sight of Coran's car outside had prepared him for the prospect of meeting a visitor, and he had managed to smooth a veneer of urbanity over the venom in his eyes, and the hard line of his mouth.

'Why, Nick,' she said, going over to him, inwardly shrinking, 'I thought you would have been at the grand farewell ball tonight. And you missed it—the social highlight of the convention. This *is* a surprise.' She tried to lift her voice in welcome, but knew that she failed miserably.

'Oh, I decided to skip the ball,' he said carelessly. 'and I left after the final symposium.' He glanced at his watch. 'Made good time, too.' He bent and kissed her cheek, a gesture which she knew to be for the benefit of Coran, who had risen.

Roz felt the imprint of his lips like a sting, and after a moment she forced herself to move slowly away. 'Nick, this is Coran Rivers. He's interested in some of my stock. Coran, my husband.'

The two men shook hands. 'I'm always pleased to meet my wife's business associates,' said Nick smoothly. 'It's a testimonial of her solvency.' As Coran laughed politely, he went on, 'Now, let me get you another drink.' He moved over to the table behind the sofa and lifted the lid of the decanter.

Coran made a firm negating gesture of his hand. 'Thank you, but no. I must be on my way. I was about to leave, anyway.'

'Oh, must you?' Roz was desperate to defer the moment when she must face Nick alone and the anger that she knew must be blazing within him. 'Coffee, perhaps? And a sandwich? It won't take a moment.'

Coran laughed. 'My dear girl, after that dinner I won't be able to look at food for several days, probably, thanks all the same.'

'And—er—about the pedlar doll, I think I might be able to arrange for you to see it tomorrow,' Roz pursued, fighting against the undertow which was drawing her closer and closer to the vortex of Nick's anger. 'In fact, I could telephone Mr Powell now and fix an appointment.'

'Oh, I'm sure that's not necessary, Roz. Having seen your stock, I've every confidence in you. If you would open the deal on my behalf, then telephone me. That's what I was about to say when your husband arrived.'

'Yes, I'll do that.' Roz was aware of Nick following this conversation with a sardonic smile flickering across his mouth. He knows that I'm playing for time, she thought dully, and he's enjoying it. It gives him a sense of power. Then she straightened briskly, reminding herself that he *had* no power over her. He had broken their agreement, going off like that with Gabriella under her very eyes. 'Fine, then, Coran,' she said. 'I'll telephone you tomorrow evening.'

'Goodnight,' Coran said to Nick. ''I hope that we'll meet again.'

'I hope so, too,' Nick said carelessly. 'You must dine with us one evening. Mind how you go. There's a hell of a storm blowing up.' The glance he flashed at Roz indicated that he wasn't speaking only of the weather.

But she was past caring. Let him do his worst.

She stood in the doorway for a moment, watching Coran drive away, then when the tail-lights had disappeared round the curve of the road she squared her shoulders and went back into the sitting-room.

Nick was still standing at the sofa table; his face, underlit by the lamp, seemed like a primitive carving of a mask. Only a small muscle under his cheekbone moved, flicking rhythmic shadows across the hard planes, and his hooded eyes concealed their expression.

He poured himself a large whisky and said in a low, ominous voice, 'Well?'

'Well, *what*?' Roz's voice was cold, although the mounting fury inside her felt like a molten core. If he thought he was going to intimidate her by his premature return in a mood calculated to frighten her, then he could think again!

'Haven't we got some talking to do?' he rasped, raising his glass and draining it.

'Oh, dear, *must* we?' She injected a note of boredom into her voice and feigned a yawn. 'I'm tired, and I'm sure you must be, too. And besides, I have nothing to say to you, Nick. And to be absolutely truthful I'm not very interested in whatever it is that you want to talk about.'

'I see,' he drawled. 'So you have nothing to say? Not even an apology for walking out on me the way you did?'

'Did I make you feel foolish? Oh, poor Nick,' she murmured. Then her voice crisped. 'I left you a note.'

'So you did.' His eyes narrowed dangerously to a golden glitter. 'And very succinct it was; it told me that you had had enough.'

'And I had. More than enough, if you want to know.' She intended to stifle the intensity of her emotions and walk out of the room calmly, but in spite of her bravado she felt Nick's presence growing to fill the space between them, crowding and dominating her. She stared back at him defiantly.

'Let me assure you that you didn't make a fool of me,' he whipped out. 'I simply said that you'd had to come home because of a sudden business deal which came up—a reason they all accepted. But to resume—at the risk of seeming repetitive, Rosamund, might I remind you of our arrangement? As my wife, you were expected to stay until the close of the convention.' His voice sharpened suddenly. 'And you know it, damn you. But you reneged.'

Roz's head snapped back in amazement as she took a step towards him, anger surging through her blood like a vigorous life force. '*I* reneged? Oh, come on! For heaven's sake, don't underestimate my intelligence, Nick. Don't try loading the guilt on to my shoulders when *you* were the one who ——'

'Ah!' he said on a note of triumph. 'I *thought* I recognised the lie of the land.'

'What on earth are you talking about?' she breathed, her eyebrows lifting. 'Stop trying to be obscure and clever. *You* violated that damned, depressing, unbearable contract we had, not I!'

'You *do* surprise me.' The change in his voice to a velvet murmur seemed more menacing than his asperity. His eyebrows rose fractionally as his glance idled over her, lingering on the breasts that stirred the soft folds of her emerald silk shirt before moving down, as if mentally stripping her of all her clothing, reminding her of the movements of his hands two nights ago. How dared he? she stormed silently. The wave of sensuality radiating from his insolent stare threatened to engulf her. She felt her body growing hot under the torment of his eyes as she tried to outface him. 'Do you mean to tell me, Rosamund, that you weren't willing? Are you suggesting—oh, surely not—that I—*raped* you?' he asked softly.

She gasped at the sheer unexpectedness of his remark. She flung up her head. 'I mean that——' Then she bit off the remainder. If she told him the truth—how much the sight of him and Gabriella hurrying out of the hotel as if they couldn't wait to be alone had hurt her, mocking all her romantic, optimistic hopes—then she merely exposed her own vulnerability. He would assume that she had walked out because of jealousy; that she cared enough about him to resent Gabriella. How that would feed his ego! Why give him that satisfaction?

And, a little voice inside her pointed out reasonably, had actually *seeing* him with Gabriella made any real difference? Roz had known what he was like when she had married him, and had been prepared for his peccadilloes; she had even thought that she was sufficiently armoured against them. But she wasn't. She knew that now. But why tell him? He would simply stare at her in amazement and laugh, pointing out the factor in their agreement which allowed him to do more or less what he liked.

Nick was drumming his fingers impatiently. 'Well?' he prompted. 'It seems to be taking you a long time to get your words together. You were going to explain exactly what you did mean.'

'I meant—that—what happened at the hotel that night was a mistake,' she mumbled. 'Not rape, exactly, but—yes—a big mistake.'

He turned away quickly and poured himself another drink. 'I see. Well, yes,' he added coldly, 'the possibility that you would see it that way had crossed my mind. As I've already said, I recognised the lie of the land. After all, I've been there before.' He took a long pull at his whisky, his gaze never leaving her face. 'Do you remember that other time, Rosamund?' His voice softened into a creamy tenderness that made her want to scream. 'Do you remember that night that began here, in this very room? And ended in your bed? Do you remember how you——?'

'Stop it!' she shouted. 'I don't want reminding of something I've been trying to forget for the past two years.'

'Your first time,' he went on inexorably. 'You seemed so young, so—untouched. Tender and wondering, endearingly pure, yet eager and shyly adventurous when——'

'Shut up! Stop it. Please!' She was mortified to hear tears in a voice which was intended to convey only a cold loathing. 'Are you the kind of man who clocks up his sexual experiences, gloating and pawing them over afterwards? Does that give you some kind of kick? Speaking for myself, I regretted that night. Bitterly.'

'Oh, you made that abundantly clear,' Nick drawled through tight lips. 'You were up and away to—Chester, wasn't it?—just as soon as your parochial little soul had reasserted itself. That's why I say I've been here before. I'm familiar with the scenario. For heaven's sake, what's wrong with you, Rosamund? Have you got some kind of hang-up that stops you from admitting that——'

'Spare me your psychology,' she shot back. 'I have no hang-ups.'

'That's a matter of opinion,' he retorted. 'From where I stand, it looks very much as if you have. Perhaps in your next reincarnation you'll come on earth as a praying mantis and have the satisfaction of actually devouring the male after the act. Not simply walking away as if nothing had happened that was worth remembering.'

'Oh, I can see why it suits you to talk that way,' Roz scoffed. 'Am I supposed to be grateful that you actually deigned to make love to me? Do you think you're giving a girl a big, shining moment? It might hurt you to hear this, Nick, but you're not completely unforgettable, you know.'

'Now, who's talking psychology?' he flashed. 'And you're quite wrong. However, I can see that it's no good pursuing the topic.' Then, with a sudden change of subject which she found disconcerting, he said spikily, 'And just where does this Coran Rivers fit in? I return from a hectic three days and a long haul to find him sitting in my chair, drinking my brandy, and making reference to the dinner at which, presumably, he had the pleasure of the company of my wife who walked out on me. So just who is he?'

'Wasn't it obvious? I'm doing business with him.'

'Really?' Nick slurred. Roz wondered if he was slightly drunk; the whiskies had been large, and he had almost finished his third. 'Now I just wonder,' he murmured, eyeing her shrewdly, 'if *he* was the real reason you left Beauchamp Gorse.'

'Of course not. I didn't even know that——'

'And,' Nick went on smoothly, 'I'm also wondering what *your* reaction would be if the position were reversed. I mean, supposing I walked out on you, and you returned to find me enjoying a tête-à-tête with a reasonably presentable female, and I explained her away by saying that she was a business associate. Would you believe me?'

'That's easy,' Roz retorted. 'In a word—no.'

'Yet you expect me to believe you, apparently,' he remarked thoughtfully.

A flash of lightning lit the room luridly for a second, followed by an explosion of thunder. The last of Roz's self-control snapped. 'I don't give a damn what you believe or don't believe,' she spat. 'Can't you get that into your head? What you do, and what you think, doesn't matter to me. But the comparison doesn't apply. The reason that *your* explanation would ring false is because *you* have a reputation, Nick. I'm sure you don't need reminding of that. I learned of it the very first night we met at Ilona's party. But in the weeks that followed, like a fool I chose to ignore or excuse it. But I'm not likely to be so blind again. And now, if you don't mind, I'm going to bed.'

'Damn you,' he whispered. 'Damn you to hell and back. You've got no ——'

'And if all you have to add are profanities, then I'll say goodnight.'

She closed the door softly behind her and went towards the stairs. Then she jumped in fright as she heard his glass shatter against the door behind her, and the tinkle of fragments on the stone-flagged floor.

Quickly she undressed, her fingers fumbling as she dealt with hooks and zipper. Her whole body was shaken by a trembling which she couldn't control. Clenching her teeth against their chattering, she got into bed and lay still. She had seen Nick angry before, but never with such a degree of savagery. Yet even then, just for a few moments, a blatant, brutal sensuality had emanated from him, homing in on her as if she were his target, and exciting her despite herself.

The front door slammed, paralysing her thoughts for a split second before she breathed a sigh of relief. He had gone out—presumably walking as she hadn't heard his car. Once he had told her that if he had a lot on his mind he found walking therapeutic; it recharged his batteries, he had said.

She lay for a while listening for his return, but then she fell into an uneasy sleep. When she awoke in the morning she saw that the clothes she had left at Beauchamp Gorse, including the lovely fishtail dress, had been dumped unceremoniously just inside her bedroom door. So he had come back.

CHAPTER NINE

THREE weeks later Roz slammed her car door behind her and ran towards the house, drawing up the collar of her Burberry against the rain. The climbing rose that clung to the walls had been stripped of its blooms by the high winds, and now the petals lay in a pink mash along the grey stone footings. The weather reflected her mood, grey and depressed, and the July evening sky lay like a bruise over the green dale.

Lights were on in the kitchen and hall, so at least someone was home—it might be Nick or it could be Ewan; she didn't look in the garage to find out. Grey Garth seemed less like a home than a transit camp these days, she thought regretfully. The men came and stayed or left as their working lives demanded, and she was the only constant factor in the household.

In the cloakroom off the hall Roz hung up her damp coat and ran a comb quickly through her rain-misted hair. This particular patch of her life—since the convention—seemed like a long frost. Each day the ice grew a little thicker, less penetrable, and the atmosphere between her and Nick a little colder.

He had adapted one of the spare bedrooms as a study-cum-office, and had brought over a large mahogany desk from Meronthorpe, together with a pair of comfortable club chairs, a couple of pictures, a small television set and a sophisticated music system. Sometimes when Roz passed the door she would hear him dictating into a machine, at other times she heard only music. And at those times she had a lunatic impulse to join him, for music had been a bond between them, but always she resisted; the door, although slightly ajar, seemed to proclaim as clearly as if the words had been painted on it, 'No admittance'. She wondered if the strains of Mozart or Rossini echoed a happy mood, or did he, too, feel the misery of the impasse as keenly as she did, and was he simply trying to cheer himself? She had no way of knowing.

Even Ewan had lost his easy, relaxing aimlessness, being engrossed in the preparation of notes for his lecture tours as well as the pursuit of contracts. But that was, at least, one thing to be thankful for; he looked brighter and more purposeful than he had in months. At last he seemed to have come to terms with Lisa's death, Roz thought, as she dried her hands. And although he still spoke of his fiancée it was without that agonised, inward-looking remorse which Roz had found so poignant.

When he was in the house she and Nick managed somehow to sustain a note approaching normality, but as Ewan had taken to staying in York quite often and was applying himself to his work with a thoroughness of which even Nick approved, Roz sometimes felt that she and her brother rarely exchanged more than a hundred words before he went off again. Perhaps, she thought, with a wry grimace, Ewan feels that he's being diplomatic in leaving Nick and me alone to enjoy our first magic months of wedded bliss... It was a good thing that Ewan was so absorbed, or surely he would have been more perceptive.

In a sense it was a blessing that Coran Rivers had bought so much of her stock, for her search for replacements took her over a wide area and her days were full, if not always fruitful.

She hung up the towel and crossed the hall. As she went through the sitting-room she saw that a bright fire burned in the grate. That could only mean Nick, she realised, her heart dipping.

He was in the kitchen, halving a small melon.

'I'm back,' she said tonelessly. 'Sorry I'm late. You didn't bargain on having to prepare your own meals, did you?'

He cocked a reflective eyebrow as he deftly scooped out the seeds. 'There are more important issues that I didn't bargain on either,' he remarked calmly.

She ignored that remark. To have asked him to explain it would only have provoked another bitter altercation, and she couldn't cope with that tonight. 'Let me do that,' she said, reaching for an apron.

He turned and looked at her then. 'Why not go up and have a bath?' he said after a moment. 'You look all in. I'll do supper. Oh,' he went on, seeing her expression change, 'I'm not above grilling a steak and tossing a salad. And if I really stretch myself I can even open a bottle of wine.'

She looked at him uncertainly for a moment, but he seemed engrossed in refilling the pepper-mill. She felt an overwhelming weakness, a need to dissolve into the kind of soft, cleansing tears that would wash away all the bitterness. She needed to be in his arms. It was as simple as that, as complicated as that!

She turned away and took a long minute to hang the apron back on its hook. 'I'm sure a bath would help,' she muttered. 'And thank you, Nick . . .'

'Well,' he said bluntly, 'I'm not such a heartless devil that I can't see when you've had a rotten day. Now go on up. Supper in twenty minutes. All right?'

She lay in the warm, scented water, feeling some of the day's frustrations seep away. Then the door opened. 'Dry martini,' Nick said. He didn't look at her, but simply set down the glass on the edge of the bath and disappeared. Those stupid, futile tears threatened her again. Fool, she hissed at herself, braced by the dry astringency of the drink. Don't be seduced by his sudden show of caring; it's part of his nature, that inbuilt charm that usually helps him to achieve his ends. It probably amuses him to soften you up. It's a challenge to his ego. Remember Beauchamp Gorse! Remember that the night which you valued so highly for a few hours meant *nothing* to him!

She tossed back the martini quickly and coughed, then she turned on the cold shower, afterwards drying herself briskly with one of Nick's huge, rough towels. She was toned up now, toughened, armoured...

He had laid places at one end of the long dining-table, so that they faced each other across the crystal candlesticks. By her plate was a single pink rosebud, one that had miraculously escaped the ravages of the recent storms. For a moment Roz's resolution was threatened, then she said lightly, 'How nice all this looks! Perhaps you ought to do it more often. Maybe I should make a point of not getting home until you're ravenously hungry and have decided to fend for yourself.'

'I thought you probably *had* made a point of it,' he said blandly, after a moment.

'Nothing so petty!' she laughed. 'My lateness tonight was unintentional and unavoidable,' she added formally.

He came round to the side of her chair to fill her glass, and his arm brushed her shoulder lightly for a moment. A little ripple ran through her as she stared at his hand, the long, capable fingers, the little glinting hairs as his wrist tilted. She had only to turn her head and her face would lie against his strong chest. She had only to draw his head down and kiss him as she had that morning in the drive and he would respond like the red-blooded, sensual animal that he was. Or would he? How deep did his steel go? How many of his thoughts were with Gabriella? Anyway, that kind of purely physical response was not enough. She leaned away from him and picked up her spoon. 'What a perfect melon this is,' she said brightly.

After the meal he sent her into the sitting-room while he made the coffee. Roz kicked off her shoes and stretched out on the sofa with a sense of well-being. He had done everything exactly right this evening. He must have divined her mood immediately she went into the kitchen, and seen what was needed. But why had he bothered? Could it be that his long-standing affair with Gabriella was now over? But, if it were, what difference did that make? He was still the same old Nick. The thought-line was too involved to pursue in her present mood. She wouldn't come up with any answers, anyway, for Nick was too complex a man to offer easy solutions. So forget it, she told herself, gazing into the fire through half-closed eyes. Sufficient unto the day...

He handed her a cup of coffee, lifted her feet and sat down at the end of the sofa, replacing her feet so that they rested on his thighs. She felt something inside her shimmer then recoil. 'Talking business before a meal isn't a good idea,' he murmured. 'Feeling a bit better now?'

She took a sip of her coffee, choked a little, then said, 'Yes. And again, thank you.'

'You've had a bad day. Tell me.'

She made a little *moue*, shaking back the glossy, blackbird-wing hair. 'Ugh...frustrating. On my way out to the auction I saw your old Nanny Berridge waiting for the bus. It was raining, so I made a detour and took her into the village to get her arthritis prescription. She had some shopping to do, so we did it and I took her home. By which time, of course, I was running late.' She watched Nick's eyes narrow as he lit a cigar. 'So I took a short cut and got behind a tractor on a very narrow road and... Oh, well, the crux of the matter is that by the time I got to the auction the basketwork doll's pram I was after had been sold, and also the box of dolls' shoes.'

'Dolls' shoes?' Nick grinned, exhaling a plume of fragrant blue smoke. 'Who on earth would have a box of dolls' shoes to sell?'

Roz shrugged. 'Perhaps they were discovered among some old stock in a shop that's recently closed down. That kind of thing does happen, you know. In the trade we regard it as a bonus—something new on the market that hasn't been through several dealers' hands, each adding their profit mark-up. So then I decided to go and see a few contacts, but there was nothing that interested me at the right price. After that I went along to see a man who telephoned me last week.'

'And he was out,' Nick said, one hand idly caressing the slim arch of her foot.

'No.' Grimly Roz kept her mind on the subject, trying to tamp down the *frissons* his touch aroused in her. 'He was in. But what he had to offer was so damaged and tatty that I had to tell him, as politely as possible, that age isn't the only consideration in my business. Condition, too, is important. It wasn't very pleasant. He probably needed the money, or perhaps he'd thought that my being a woman meant I wouldn't hold out against him. He was very persistent, then he turned quite nasty about my wasting his time.' She edged her foot away slightly, and his hand was still. 'So there you have it. A high mileage and nothing to show for it.'

'Still, you did Nanny Berridge a favour,' Nick said.

Roz smiled. 'Well, if a good deed shines in a naughty world, it certainly didn't light up my day.'

'Oh, we none of us win them all, to voice a cliché,' Nick said idly.

'I'll bet you do, though,' The swift retort came before Roz could stop it.

'You should know better than to think that,' he murmured. 'You of all people.'

She stared at him for a moment, then her gaze dropped away. 'Where's Ewan?' she asked, breaking a silence that pulsated between them, heavy with baffling, intricate undertones.

'Oh, I forgot. He telephoned, and he's staying in York. Gone to a jazz concert with someone called Denny.'

Roz wished that Nick would go and sit in his usual chair. His nearness trapped her. But no way was she going to allow him to get any closer, only to drop her again when it was convenient. She sat up sharply, swinging her legs to the floor and leaning forward to put her coffee-cup on the tray.

'Did *you* have a good day?' she asked lamely, seeking refuge in conversation.

Nick sat back, his fingers interlaced behind his head. 'Excellent, and I'm hoping to put some work Ewan's way.'

Roz bit off a remark at this evidence of Nick's sudden confidence in Ewan. 'I'm glad he's beginning to enjoy himself again,' she said, after a moment.

'I got the impression that Denny was a girl,' said Nick.

'Oh, great. But you were saying—about your day?'

'Mmm. I've decided to diversify a little. And,' he added with a quizzical sideways glance, 'being a married man, I think it's time to bring more work nearer home. A smallish firm of clothing manufacturers was in the doldrums, so, in return for a seat on their board and a great deal of say in their affairs, I've injected a fair amount of capital into their company. They're turning over to making high-quality leisure-wear.' He drew on his cigar. 'So you see, my dear, I'm hoping to cut down on all my travelling.'

Roz's face was carefully blank as she said, 'It sounds very interesting. And where does Ewan fit in?'

'Well, I did a lot of persuasive talking today. They need a complete new image, something with—verve, impact... So I'm going to ask Ewan to come up with a new logo, redesign all their packaging, letterheads, labels...the lot. Their image is tarnished, dowdy. I want something really fresh and vigorous, something that—*zings*. Ewan's got imagination and flair, and it'll be interesting to see his ideas.'

'I'm sure he'll welcome the opportunity,' Roz said, her eyes shining.

'And while marketing isn't my province I do have the obvious outlets for leisure-wear, so I'll be able to keep a finger on the pulse to some extent. Of course, the thing's in its infancy yet, and we need new designers, new fabric-suppliers, a big, adventurous advertising campaign. But all that will be taken care of at the right time. So, you see, altogether I've had a very rewarding day.'

'In complete contrast to mine,' Roz said ruefully. She frowned. 'What's really bothering me is that I promised to mount a little exhibition at a garden party in aid of the children's home over at Durswell. But since Coran took most of my stock I'm left with a couple of children's chairs and three dolls and very little else. When I agreed to do it I didn't foresee there'd be such a run on my stock, and I haven't a hope now of getting a decent show together in just over a week.'

Nick nodded. 'Mmm. Well, why don't you see what there is at Meronthorpe? There are boxes of stuff in the attics. I'm sure they'll yield something. I know for certain that there's an ancient rocking-horse, though I can't vouch for the condition of its mane and tail.'

Roz leaned forward eagerly. 'Oh, may I? That would be marvellous! Oh, but wouldn't Rolfe object? I mean—rummaging about among the relics of the Martel dynasty——'

Nick threw back his head and laughed. 'What an odd picture you have of the Martels,' he said. 'And I had thought it was just I who bothered you!' Then he went on more seriously, 'I'm sure my father would be only too pleased to lend his support to a worthy cause. I shouldn't think he ever gives a thought to all that old junk. I'm sure we'll find something.'

'Oh, Nick—I...' Roz's words died. A will-o'-the-wisp, precarious happiness stretched out frail threads inside her. How pleasant life would be if all evenings were like this one! But, on second thoughts, those gossamer threads made up a trap as damaging as if they were steel. And this was the moment to place herself beyond the treacherous influence of the warm light in his eyes, the relaxed, sensual, amused mouth, the seduction that lay in the way he spoke her name, the mood that he had created tonight.

She stood up quickly. 'I'm really grateful. You may have got me out of an embarrassing situation. Could we go over to Meronthorpe tomorrow and take a look?' Her expression was bright and enquiring, her smile impersonal but agreeable.

'Tomorrow? It'll have to be in the morning, then. I go away in the afternoon. Three days here in England, then on to the States for a week or so.'

'Oh? You didn't tell me.' She bent to pick up the tray, blanking out an unexpected stab of disappointment.

'I didn't know myself definitely, until today. Why, Rosamund,' he said tauntingly, 'don't tell me that you're going to miss me?'

'I wasn't going to tell you any such thing,' she retaliated. 'Your comings and goings are part of our deal.'

For a moment there was a prickling silence, then he said, his voice throbbing, 'Does *nothing* I say get through to you?'

She looked at him quickly. His eyes were narrowed and intense, his jaw set in a hard line. 'Yes,' she answered reasonably, 'it's got through to me. You're going away again. What's so special about that?'

'Oh, nothing. I should have known better than to ask,' he said bitterly.

'You've lost me, I'm afraid,' Roz said smoothly, balancing the tray on her hip and opening the door. 'I'll see to these, then I'm going to bed.'

'Right. I'll go up to the office for a while. You certainly have a knack of dispelling a pleasant atmosphere. Goodnight.'

He was brisk and matter-of-fact the following morning, glancing at the clock, and telling her to hurry. He could spare about three hours, but wanted to be on his way before twelve. He would grab a quick pub lunch on his way north.

Rolfe was surprised and pleased to see them. 'Nancy has only just taken my breakfast things away,' he said. He looked quizzically from Nick to Roz, then said, 'Is this a special occasion? I'm sure it must be; do you realise it's the first time I've seen you two together since your wedding day? It's one or the other, but never both of you.'

'Well, you know how it is,' Nick said pleasantly. 'I'm away such a lot, and then Rosamund comes. When I get back she's usually busy. Actually, it's business you have to thank for this visit because I'm off again before lunch. I'll be away for a couple of weeks.' Quickly he explained Roz's predicament. 'So with your permission we're on our way up to the attics,' he concluded.

'Take what you want, my dear,' said Rolfe, smiling at Roz. 'You might have to dig deep, though, for anything of interest. Each generation of Martels has added a layer. And when you've finished, join me for a sherry, will you?'

Up in the attic Roz surveyed the trunks and boxes with mixed dismay and anticipation. The sun was out and the succession of small rooms leading out of each other under the roof were warm, lit only by panes of glass, mist-grey and cobwebbed, let into the tiles.

'We'll never get through all this lot,' she began nervously. She was very conscious of Nick in the close, suffocating little rooms where generations of Martel servants had alternately roasted or frozen for so many years.

'They're labelled,' Nick said, brushing the dust off a tea-chest and reading aloud, 'Albums, gramophone records, magazines...' He moved to another box. 'Linen, curtains...' Then he stopped. 'This is recent stuff. Let's begin at the far end. Maybe it's in chronological order, moving forward towards the stairs.'

Ducking his head, he passed through the small connecting openings. 'Ah, this looks more like it.'

For an hour or so he and Roz knelt, peeling away brittle, biscuit-coloured paper to reveal the contents of the chests. 'I could spend days here,' Roz breathed, reluctantly laying aside a children's book of moral stories illustrated with fat, red-cheeked children. 'Oh, look!' She pulled out a small doll, then a tiny, blue-painted crib with a patchwork quilt, each piece the size of a postage stamp. 'Marvellous! And these old building blocks...'

'I'll go and get some cartons to put them in,' Nick said. 'A couple should be enough.'

While she was alone, Roz eagerly explored the contents of the boxes and trunks. She was exclaiming over a chemist's shop when Nick came back. 'Do look, Nick,' she enthused. 'All these tiny drawers, each one labelled and with its own tiny china knob, and even the big flasks and a leech jar.' She sat back on her heels, her eyes glowing. 'This is wonderful. Such a pity they have to be hidden away, though. Still,' she laughed, 'it's nice for me that they *have* been.' She watched Nick set down the cartons and take out two long, frosted glasses, and she realised how warm and thirsty she was. She smiled at him. 'Thank you,' she said. 'I seem to have been thanking you rather a lot lately.' She took a deep, cooling drink and reached into another box to take out a doll.

For a moment she stared at it without speaking. A fashion doll, made and dressed to exhibit the style of the day, it had been made in France during the last century. It was perfect, down to the detail of knitted silk stockings with tiny embroidered clocks up the sides. Lying against the doll was a small parasol of Mechlin lace with an intricately carved ivory handle.

Nick, distracted by her silence, looked up from the model of a governess cart which he had unearthed. 'Why,' he exclaimed, 'that was my mother's. I remember now—it always stood on her night-table.'

'It's exquisite,' Roz breathed, reverently re-wrapping it and putting it back in the box.

'Don't you want to show it?' His russet eyebrows lifted in surprise.

'I'd love to, but . . . knowing that it belonged to your mother makes it special. I mean . . .' She laughed uncertainly, pushing away her hair with a dusty hand, 'the others are—anonymous, but——'

'Take it,' Nick said, watching her with a half-smile. 'You have my permission. And you heard what Father said.'

'May I? Oh, lovely! It'll be the star attraction.' Roz attempted a breathless little laugh to dispel an atmosphere which had suddenly become electric, like the hush before a storm. She sat with the doll held between her hands, looking down at the fringed cape with its lining embroidered in minute stitches. Only her heartbeats seemed loud in the silence.

Slowly, as if on invisible wires, Nick's hand moved. One finger brushed her thumb with a delicacy which she sensed rather than felt. She looked up at him, her hand lifting of its own volition to meet his palm so that they seemed to share a prayer. And as she felt his warm skin against hers the atmosphere exploded into incandescence. Roz stared at him wordlessly, her eyes soft and imploring, her lips slightly parted.

'Come with me, Rosamund,' he said huskily. She felt that his gaze uncovered her very soul, revealing all the tumult of her emotions.

She couldn't speak. Their two hands melding together held a crackling charge that numbed all logical thought.

'Come with me,' he urged again.

'Today?' she whispered at last.

He shook his head impatiently. 'No...no. Meet me at the airport on Friday. Fly out to Florida with me. My schedule is prohibitively tight until then. But after Friday... We'll go to the Keys together, just the two of us. And then, perhaps, we can——'

'No!' she cried, wrenching her thoughts back to a practical plane. 'No, I can't! You know that. There's the garden party, and I can't let them down.'

His hand left hers and his mouth twisted. 'How very convenient for you.' In his low voice she heard only the biting, accusing note.

'Nick,' she faltered, 'it's—'

'Forget it.' He brushed her explanation aside. 'It was a silly question when I already knew the answer.' He took the doll from her and put it aside. 'Now,' he said briskly, 'how much more of this stuff do you want?'

She felt empty and unreal. 'Oh... I think I have enough now.'

Somehow she got through the social pleasantries over sherry with Nancy and Rolfe, and accepted an invitation for her and Nick to dine at Meronthorpe the night after Nick returned. Then he drove her back to Grey Garth to deliver the toys and pick up his luggage.

'See you in a couple of weeks or so, then,' he said casually, as she went out to the car with him. 'And Rosamund,' he went on, turning sharply to look down at her, his face wintry and austere, 'you can't run away for ever. I think it's time we——'

He broke off with a muffled curse as Anna Sloot's head appeared among the rhododendrons.

'We're back,' she announced gaily. 'Just got here. Come round for drinks. Roz, you look as if you have been up the chimney.'

Roz smiled stiffly, her mind buzzing with the implications of Nick's remark. 'Well, not quite a chimney, but almost. And sorry, Anna, but Nick's just leaving.'

'Work. Always it is work,' Anna said disgustedly. 'I wish you a safe journey then, Nick, and when you come back——'

'You and Piet will dine with us,' Nick interjected smoothly. 'We'll look forward to it.' He bent to kiss Roz, but his lips were hard and unyielding.

Roz sighed as he got into the car and waved once, then at Anna's insistence followed her through the shrubbery into the house.

Later that afternoon, as Roz was packing away the last of the treasures yielded up by Meronthorpe, the telephone rang. At first it didn't register, for despite a task which normally she would have enjoyed wholeheartedly, she was *distrait*, her mind reaching back repeatedly to that moment in the attic when the touch of a hand had shown her that Nick was the only thing in the world that really mattered. Despite all her attempts to rationalise, love was still there, as fresh and vibrant as it had been two years ago. And just as hopeless, if not more so. Nick might be the only man in the world for her, but that was no reason to be blinded to his real self.

She sighed. Even so, as she packed the tissue-wrapped toys carefully, her imagination could not resist offering her tiny pictures, cameos, dreams—of a shared and happy future. Nick's behaviour last evening, for instance... He had been so thoughtful, so tender, so completely on her side... It was a taste of how things *might* have been. And today—that brief, brilliant explosion of passion answering passion through the innocent medium of two palms touching. Just that... and yet so much.

She stood up, wearily pushing away her hair with the back of her hand. How did one blank out such vivid, luminous images? Only by reminding oneself of other moments of humiliation and bitterness...

She heard the telephone then, shrilling across her confusion. Her heart leapt. It just might be Nick. What was it he had wanted to say when Anna appeared? Her hand was eager as she lifted the receiver.

Gabriella's voice stunned her for a moment. 'May I have a word with Nick?' the soft voice asked. 'Or has he already left?'

Roz swallowed. After a moment she said steadily, 'Yes, I'm afraid you've missed him. He went about a couple of hours ago.'

'Oh, dear.' Gabriella paused, then said, 'Have you any idea where he's going?'

'Not really. Here and there, he said, on a tight schedule. Oh, he did mention going north today.' With a sickening pang Roz recalled that Gabriella ran a holiday centre in the Lake District. Was that where Nick was heading? She shut her eyes and leaned against the wall.

'I see.' Gabriella's voice was expressionless. 'Well, thank you anyway, Rosamund.' The fact that Gabriella shared Nick's use of Roz's full name seemed to em-

phasise the link between them. 'Incidentally,' Gabriella
went on, 'I was so sorry you had to dash away from the
convention. Nick said that some pressing business had
come up.'

'Ye-es. As a matter of fact,' Roz extemporised, 'I'm
getting a little exhibition together and . . .' She bit off her
words. Why bother to lie to Gabriella, of all people?
She owed her no explanation, false or otherwise.

'It sounds fascinating. I should love to see some of
your dolls. And why don't you and Nick come up here
some time? We really ought to get together soon.'

Why? thought Rosamund. To make things easier for
you and Nick? A kind of *menage à trois* where, to all
appearances, we're all great pals? Is that the way you
and Nick hope to play it?

'Yes,' she muttered feebly. 'I'm sure that would be—
nice. Well, if you'll excuse me, I'm terribly busy. Sorry
I can't help. Goodbye now.' Violently she crashed down
the receiver. If she had been in danger of succumbing
to all those impossibly tantalising little dreams of some
kind of future for herself and Nick, then Gabriella had
certainly averted it! Even now, at this very moment, Nick
was speeding north. Was Gabriella his journey's end?

But there wasn't a thing that Roz could do about it.
It had been written into that crass, unbearable marriage
contract.

I can't go on, she thought. I can't take any more. It
has to end. It's destroying me. When Nick comes back
I'll tell him I've tried, but I've failed. I will *not* be a
smoke-screen for his affairs. Dully she brushed away her
tears and returned to her work.

On the following Tuesday, as Roz was about to leave
the house, the telephone rang. Paul Martel's voice, raw
with anxiety, surprised her into momentary silence. 'It's
Father,' he said without preamble. 'He's not well
and——'

'Nick's away,' Roz said quickly, 'and I don't——'

'Yes, I know he's away. But . . . Roz, I left my cricket-bag at the top of the stairs and Nancy fell. She's broken her leg. The doctor came and he rang for an ambulance and——'

'I see,' Roz said crisply. 'I'll come over right away. I can stay at Meronthorpe until we sort something out. What's wrong with Rolfe?'

'A chill, that's all. But the doctor's not too happy. Oh, hell, I don't know anything about illness. And I've got to get to the office. I've a client coming over from Lincoln and——'

'Don't worry, Paul.' Roz knew that he had recently been taken into partnership with a firm of solicitors. 'Give me about half an hour to get some things together, then I'll be with you.'

She wrote a note for Ewan, who was due back that day, packed a bag and drove over to Meronthorpe. Nancy had already left in the ambulance, Paul told her. 'But obviously she can't look after Father,' he said worriedly. 'Oh, lord, I wish Nick were here to sort things out.'

'I'll try and get a message to him somehow,' Roz said reassuringly. 'But don't worry. I'll see if I can arrange for a temporary nurse. You get along to the office, Paul. There's nothing you can do.'

His frown eased. 'Thanks, Roz. You're a cracker. Nancy knows that you'll be here, and she'll be phoning you later with some instructions. She's going to stay with her sister until she can get about again. And the doctor will call in to have another look at Rolfe this afternoon. I'd better be off now, or I'll never make it in time.'

Roz tiptoed into Rolfe's room. The atmosphere there had changed subtly from that morning, exactly one week ago, when she, dusty and disorientated, had sat here sipping Rolfe's dry sherry and pretending to take an in-terest in the conversation. Now the room held the essence of age and sickness, and Rolfe, asleep, looked frail and insubstantial as the shallow breaths he drew hardly stirred the covers.

She sat down by the bed and gently took the hot, dry hand, as if by some kind of osmosis she could channel her own youth and health into the blue veins.

Later Nancy telephoned to tell Roz of Rolfe's little foibles which she had always pandered to. 'I'm so sorry,' she said distractedly. 'This is all most unfortunate, and just when Mr Martel's not well. But in my present state it's——'

'Don't worry,' Roz reassured her. 'Everything's under control. We're none of us indispensable you know,' she teased, 'so you just concentrate on yourself. The doctor's arranging for a nurse to take over.' She did not think it necessary to add to Nancy's worries by explaining that the nurse would not be free until early the following week. In the meantime, a visiting nurse would call in twice each day. A nursing-home was out of the question in view of Rolfe's frequently expressed intent to spend the rest of his days in the home where he was born, and where his wife had died.

It was only when Roz was riffling through her diary to make sure that she was free of any definite business commitments that the first tiny shock struck. Quickly she flicked over the pages again. She had never given the possibility of pregnancy a thought, but now she saw that it was a distinct probability. At first she couldn't think straight as a burning heat flooded her. Was it possible? That night in Beauchamp Gorse? The night when Nick had told her that she belonged with him, and she had thought it was an affirmation of love? Only later had she realised that he was merely staking a claim as her husband. Out of those few hours could come a new being's whole life?

She shook her head as if to clear it, when she heard the tinkle of Rolfe's bedside bell, and for a while she had to push her own problems out of her mind.

But one thing was sure; now more than ever it was important to end this marriage. To bring up a child in the atmosphere that prevailed between herself and Nick was insupportable. Maybe if she told Nick about the baby he would be prepared to change his ways for the child's sake. But that wasn't enough and, in a sense, it placed too much responsibility on one who was, as yet, only a minute promise of life.

A divorce would solve all her problems, and, although later Nick would have the usual access to his child, Roz would build a life for the two of them—a happy, secure life undisturbed by the undercurrents which seemed inevitable whenever she and Nick were together.

She would have a pregnancy test, of course, although instinctively she was certain of the result. In the meantime, her work was cut out here at Meronthorpe.

When Paul came home late that afternoon he was relieved to see that Roz had everything under control. 'There is one thing bothering me, though,' Roz told him as their meal was served. Rolfe slept in the room above, but Roz ate quickly, anxious to get back to him. 'I've promised to give an exhibition of antique toys at the garden party in Durswell on Saturday. I was wondering if Nanny Berridge could come and sit with your father. I know she isn't very agile, but——'

'Don't worry about that,' Paul said warmly. 'I'll sit with the old man, and the nurse will be calling, won't she?'

'Yes. And I'll only be away for about four hours.'

'Well, then. It's the least I can do. You've been wonderful, Roz. Nick's a lucky bloke. Any news from him, incidentally?'

'No. I rang his head office, and if he calls them as he sometimes does when he's abroad, they'll tell him about the situation here. That's all we can do, I think. Apparently he hired a car in Miami, so he could be almost anywhere.'

Paul looked at her curiously. 'I would have thought that he would phone *you* when he goes away.'

Roz smiled. 'Too busy, I expect. Besides, he knows I'll be here when he gets back.' But this is the last time I will be, she added silently, her thoughts reverting to the future which she must plan. She dabbed her lips with her napkin and stood up. 'Have my coffee sent upstairs, will you, Paul? I want to get back to your father.'

Before she went to bed in the dressing-room opening off Rolfe's bedroom, Roz was relieved to see that his colour was a little better and his breathing more relaxed. He was awake but drowsy, and for a time she sat with him, talking quietly about anything that came into her mind which didn't demand either his concentration or his answer. And when at last he slept she went back into her own room.

But solitude set the treadmill of her mind in motion again, and in a resolute attempt to escape her own thoughts she went downstairs, picked up the daily paper from the hall table where it lay, still folded, and took it up. The crossword, at least, might provide a way out of the maze of futile thinking.

After half an hour there was one clue unsolved: a quotation from Swinburne...

She recalled seeing a volume of Swinburne in Nick's old room, and the search for the right answer would occupy some more time. It was almost one o'clock, but she was as far from sleep as she had ever been.

Tucking her legs under her in the big armchair, she flipped the pages, scanning the verses quickly. Then a photograph fell into her lap, face down. In neat, angular script was the message, 'Deya. Weren't we happy here?' Slowly, and almost certain of what she would see, Roz turned it over. Gabriella's face looked back at her. Above the laughing, tilted face, the arching bough of a lemon tree dangled its bright fruit against an intense blue sky. Gabriella was wearing a simple black top with bootlace straps above brief shorts in hot colours of lime and fuchsia, turquoise, and strong, vibrant orange. Her pale hair looking almost white, blowing back from the vivacious, radiant, darkly tanned face, gave a life and movement to the photograph, seeming to bring Gabriella into this very room. Roz remembered the other poem, the one she had read in Nick's room at Grey Garth, where he had marked a few lines, something about hair being twined . . . 'in all my waterfalls' . . .

For a long moment Roz sat staring down, absently reaching over the arm of her chair, into her handbag, for a handkerchief, and unconsciously wiping away the tears that began to gather.

Then gradually the unhappiness of the past months welled up inside her. She put the photograph down on the broad arm of the chair, lay down with her head on it and gave herself up to the sobs that threatened to tear her body apart.

At last, exhausted, she crept into bed. Her emotions spent, surely now she would sleep, she reasoned numbly. But when she did the nightmare came. She half awoke, trying desperately to struggle into full consciousness, dragging herself away from the threat of that terrifying wave. Whimpering and shaking, she tried to comfort herself with the knowledge that it was only a dream. But now there were no strong arms to help her, no deep, soothing voice to smooth away her fright. There never would be, she realised, ever again.

Drearily she belted on her housecoat and went into Rolfe's room. He was awake. 'I heard you,' he whispered, 'and I couldn't do anything.'

'I'm all right now,' she murmured, lifting his head and turning his pillow before settling him again. 'It was a bad dream. I'll sit with you for a while, though.'

The nightlight gave the room a ghostly, unreal glimmer. The memory of that rearing curl of water was still close, and now, seeing it again in retrospect, Roz fancied that its colours were those of Gabriella's tiny shorts.

CHAPTER TEN

ON the following Saturday, as Roz set up her table under the spread of a copper beech tree, her mood was more buoyant than it had been for days. Relieved of the muted atmosphere of Meronthorpe and the Gabriella-haunted torment of her mind, the garden party provided a temporary escape. The warm sun filtered through the thick canopy of leaves overhead, and the green sweep of lawn buzzed with activity, laughter and talk as other stall-holders arranged their stands with jars of preserves, bric-a-brac, country crafts and nearly new items.

Rolfe had continued to improve, and Roz had left him propped up on pillows listening to Paul reading from his favourite Jerome novel.

The result of her pregnancy test was positive and, now that she had made some tentative plans for a future which excluded Nick and the conflict that had bedevilled the last months, she was able to think of the baby with the first stirrings of happy anticipation. If she couldn't have Nick in the complete and fulfilling way she had once so foolishly dreamed of, then surely to bear his child was to have some unique part of him.

Acquaintances came and went, stopping to admire Roz's display and asking after Rolfe's health. Strangers came, too, interested in the array of toys, and Roz found herself talking freely and informatively, an authority on her subject. One very elegant woman lingered for a long time, then said, 'I was wondering if you would consider coming to speak to my ladies' luncheon group.' As Roz raised surprised eyebrows, she went on, 'I know it would be one of the highlights of our calendar. May I put it to the committee, then get in touch with you?'

Roz laughed, then hesitated for a moment. But why not? Public speaking would be a new experience, and surely it was such occasions as this that would lay the foundations of a different and interesting life. 'Thank you,' she said. 'I'll give you my address.' She opened her handbag. She hadn't realised that Gabriella's photograph was inside. It must have fallen from the arm of the chair that night. The sight of it froze her for a moment, and she smiled automatically as she handed the woman her card.

Then she swung round, startled, as a familiar voice said sharply, 'Where did you get *that*?'

Nanny Berridge was staring at the fashion doll which was the centrepiece of the display, standing above the other toys on the stage of a model theatre which had also come from Meronthorpe.

'Isn't she lovely?' Roz said, hastily switching her mind back to the present. 'Nick's father gave me the run of the attics so that I could mount a decent show.'

'That doll belonged to Mrs Martel,' Miss Berridge said baldly.

'Yes, I know,' Roz answered, puzzled by the older woman's strange manner. 'Nick told me, but he suggested that I bring it. Is something wrong?' She pulled out the stool from behind her stand, and Miss Berridge sat down heavily.

'No, no... Not wrong. It just came as a shock, that's all. Seeing it again, so sudden. I hid it, you see, at the bottom of a box in the far attic years ago, after Mrs Martel died.'

'Let me bring you a cool drink,' Roz murmured, worried by Miss Berridge's agitation. 'Are you *sure* you're all right?'

'Yes. Yes, thank you, my dear. It's just that it brought everything back to me as if it were yesterday.' She was silent for a few moments, then she said musingly, 'I'd told her not to ride. "It won't do that baby any good," I said. But she laughed at me. "You're an old fusspot, Nanny," she said. "Moya's steady enough, and I want to watch the hunt pass." I told her she could see the hunt comfortably in a car, but she wouldn't have it. The mare got caught up in some wire and the mistress was thrown. She lost the baby, of course.' Miss Berridge shook her head sadly.

'How tragic,' Roz murmured.

'Aye.' Miss Berridge fetched up a heavy sigh. 'She recovered, but something seemed to have gone out of her... It was a sad time for everyone. And there were the two boys, Nick and Paul, lively as crickets. It didn't seem fair on them, the way things were at Meronthorpe. Eventually I told the master that a change of air would be good for her, and he took her off to Paris. And it worked. She came back like a bride from her honeymoon.'

Miss Berridge stopped, a slow, reminiscent smile pouching her pink cheeks. 'I well remember the day they came back, she swathed in furs and looking very chic, with presents for everyone and great big hugs for the boys. And the first thing of her own that she unpacked was that doll there. The master had bought it for her from an antique shop in Paris. She put it on her bedside-table, and that's where it stayed. "To remind me," she said to me once, "that life is for living".'

'I wish I had known her,' Roz said softly.

Miss Berridge nodded. 'So when she died six years later the first thing I did was to remove that doll. It would have reminded the master... I don't think he even noticed that it had gone. He wasn't up to noticing much in those days. And he never asked about it afterwards. Seeing it again gave me a bit of a turn.' She got up stiffly with the aid of her stick. 'It's all a long time ago now. How *is* the master? I was going to go up to the house and ask after him, but my arthritis has been bad. I wouldn't be here now if Mrs Winkworth hadn't kindly offered to bring me.'

'Paul is with his father this afternoon, and he's much better.'

'You're looking a bit peaky yourself,' Miss Berridge said in her blunt way. 'You ought to keep that husband of yours at home more often.'

Roz smiled non-committally and gave her attention to a Brownie carrying a large jar and inviting them to guess the number of peas inside.

When she arrived back at Meronthorpe, Paul met her with the news that Nick had telephoned and would be home on Monday, and it was with mixed feelings of relief and trepidation that Roz resumed her care of Rolfe.

The afternoon seemed to have tired him, and while he slept Roz unpacked the toys and returned them to the attic. For a moment she held the fashion doll thoughtfully, remembering Miss Berridge's story. Then, on impulse, she took it into Rolfe's room and placed it on the chest where he would be able to see it. During his illness he had constantly spoken of past moments; he had once told Roz that reminiscence was nature's compensation for growing old. She felt that the doll would recall happier days spent beyond the confines of this sick-room.

When Nick arrived early on Monday morning Roz was sitting with Rolfe, growing increasingly alarmed about his breathing and anxiously awaiting the doctor's visit. The nurse was due to arrive in the evening, and one of the maids was preparing the dressing-room in readiness for her.

Roz had been up since before four, and had sat in the big chair, alternately dozing and waking, and when Nick opened the door it seemed to take a moment for her tired eyes to focus properly. He came over to the bed and stood looking down at his father for a moment, his face grave.

As if sensing his son's presence, Rolfe opened his eyes slowly and smiled. 'Glad you're here,' he whispered. 'She's a wonderful nurse...' Then he drifted back into his limbo.

Roz got up and went over to the bed to straighten the sheet and brush the strong grey hair away from Rolfe's flushed forehead. Nick's nearness seemed to overpower her, and she was gripped by a paralysing shyness, but at last she had to face him.

'Thank you, Rosamund,' he said quietly, then he gave the ghost of a rueful smile. 'You see? Now it's my turn to thank you.'

He looked tired and strained despite his tan, yet she was piercingly aware of the strength that pulsed behind the serious eyes and controlled mouth, a strength which—even after the long flight and the drive home—she knew was there for them all to draw upon. 'The doctor will be here soon,' she explained softly, 'and a nurse is due to arrive late this afternoon. Things will be better then.'

'And in the meantime,' Nick said, his voice reassuringly firm, 'I'm here. Why not go home now, Rosamund? I can't begin to express my appreciation for your taking charge of things here.'

'But I could stay. There might be something I can——'

'No.' Nick came over to her and put his arm around her shoulders, drawing her close to him. He tilted up her face and said severely, 'Have a break from all this. And get some rest. You look as if you need it.'

'Well, I...' His closeness and his concern threatened a sense of panic that she fought to control. And suddenly Grey Garth offered a haven. She couldn't stay here with Nick, knowing what she was going to tell him. Clearly, this was not the moment to reveal her intentions, yet by concealing them she felt an impostor. 'Yes, all right. I will. If you need me for anything you must telephone. I'll see you—some time then.'

There was a faint sense of release in driving away from the big house. Rolfe's illness, Nick's appearance and her own misery in that little dressing-room had pressed upon her like a great weight. Sooner or later must come the reckoning with Nick, but for the present there was nothing she could do but appreciate this respite.

After Rolfe's stertorous breathing the house seemed like a quiet refuge. Ewan was in London, and she had the place to herself. A hot bath and a morning's sleep worked their cure, and afterwards, in an effort to distract her mind from her problems, she worked in the garden until the shadows lengthened and the midges started to bite. The simplicity of manual toil, the smell of the soil and the feel of handling live, growing things satisfied some need within her. Tired by the fresh air and the exercise, she slept soundly that night, not hearing the storm, and waking after nine.

She was in the kitchen making tea and toast when the doorbell rang; Nick stood there, his face set in a mould of pain that drew the lines deeply between lips and nostrils and hooded his eyes with shadow. He looked bone-weary. 'I seem to have mislaid my key,' he said tonelessly. Then, from inside his jacket, he drew out the fashion doll. 'It was a kind thought,' he went on, still in the same dead tone, 'but it won't be needed any more. Give it to your friend Rivers.'

But Roz wasn't listening. Instinctively her hands went out to him, drawing him in. 'What can I say?' she whispered. 'Oh, Nick... I'm so very, very sorry.'

Nick moved like a man in a dream. Roz saw with dazed surprise that the shoulders of his jacket were wet, and wondered where he had walked this morning. From the state of the path, it was obvious that the rain had stopped some hours ago. So had Nick, in the dawn, walked and walked the gravel paths of Meronthorpe in misery? I should have stayed, she wept inwardly. I should have been with him. I might not have helped, but at least I could have been there with him...

'Let me take your coat,' she said gently. 'I'll run a bath for you. I'll bring up some coffee, and then you must sleep. You can't go on any longer.' It struck her then that she was offering exactly the same quality of bodily comfort that Nick had offered her that last evening before he left. This was the way it should be—between man and wife. Yet they had never been man and wife in the true sense of the term. And never would be...

'You're right,' he said. 'Jet-lag catching up with me on top of everything else. It was pneumonia; he had to have oxygen, but...'

She nodded. 'If you want to, we'll talk about it later. Not now, though.'

When she heard Nick's bath-water running away, Roz took up a tray. Quickly she changed the linen on her bed, and when she heard Nick come into the small adjoining room she opened the communicating door. 'Why not sleep in here?' she suggested gently. 'It's more comfortable.' She was relieved to see that some of the greyness had left his face.

A shadow of his usual self surfaced. 'Promotion?' he murmured with the tiniest flicker of a sardonic smile.

Roz didn't answer. She went to the window and closed the curtains against the sunlight, fighting down an overpowering desire to get into bed with him, to pillow his head on her breast and warm him with her body. 'You'll feel better when you've slept,' she said shortly, and went out.

Later, when she went up for the tray, she saw that he was fast asleep, one arm flung above his head, his face peaceful. A swift rush of tears stung her eyes as she watched him for a moment. No matter how much she hardened her heart against him, even in sleep the very essence of him could get to her, twisting her heart with longing, taunting her with the thought of how things might have been if only... If only Nick hadn't been...Nick! And if only there hadn't been a Gabriella waiting in the wings for her moment to go on stage.

Pointless thinking of all that now, she scolded herself as she went downstairs. She just had to contain herself patiently until she judged the moment ripe to make the first move in shaping her future life. In the meantime it helped to keep busy, and there must be something she could do up at Meronthorpe.

When she arrived, Paul was reversing his car out of the garage. His face, too, showed a numbed strain, but he was impeccably dressed and smoothly shaved. He got out of his car and came over to kiss her. She gave him a silent, sisterly hug that said more than words.

'There's nothing I can do here,' Paul said dully. 'It's best if I go to the office and try to...occupy myself.'

Roz nodded. 'What about the nurse?' she said.

'Oh, Nick saw to that. No patient, no job. He wrote her a cheque and she left first thing to work on another case. I gathered she's very much in demand. How's Nick?'

'Shattered. I left him fast asleep.'

Paul nodded. 'I don't know how he stands the pace. He never left—Father's side. Well, I'd better be off.'

'Paul, if you want to come and stay at Grey Garth with us for a few days, you're more than welcome,' Roz began.

'Thanks, but no. I'm all right, really. Or I will be, after the funeral.'

Thoughtfully, Roz went into the house. A red-eyed maid was dusting in the hall, and there was a damp, muted atmosphere about the place. Roz said a brisk 'Good morning,' then went upstairs to Rolfe's room. Nick wouldn't have thought to issue any instructions to the staff, and it might well be that they would avoid this room unless told otherwise.

Quickly she forced herself to strip the bed and put the linen in the laundry basket. She folded the blankets and stowed than away in a chest on the landing. She flushed Rolfe's pills and medicine down the lavatory and threw the empty bottles into a bin. Then she opened his wardrobe. Someone had to do it; better that she was that person.

Without letting herself think too much about the man who had worn the green Norfolk jacket, the hopelessly old-fashioned morning dress, the hand-made brogues and patent leather pumps, she carried them up to the attic and neatly folded them into the empty trunks. The Jerome book from which Paul had been reading on the Saturday afternoon of the garden party she returned to a bookcase downstairs.

And now the room was anonymous; no trace of the man whose world it had been for so many months. She sniffed, compressing her lips, then she let the tears come as she remembered her wedding breakfast here. You see, Rolfe, she said silently, you weren't the only one to whom memories were important.

With a feeling that she had made her last farewell to him, she went out. At least Nick would be spared the horrid task of seeing to his father's clothes. Eventually they would be found by someone, but that would be after the present sorrow had passed.

The maid was still in the hall when she went down, desultorily rubbing up the big polished steel andirons in the cavernous fireplace. 'Mr Martel's room is ready for cleaning now,' Roz said quietly. 'And after that you and the rest of the staff are free. But stay close to the house, will you? I think my husband might want to see you all later.'

*   *   *

When she arrived back at Grey Garth, Nick was sitting by the open french window, staring unseeingly out at the garden. He rose when Roz came in.

'Feeling better for your sleep?' she asked shyly.

He nodded. 'I'd better get back to Meronthorpe. There are things to do.'

'I think you should eat first. No,' she lifted her hand, 'I'm not listening to any refusals. Just an omelette and some fruit. It won't take a minute.'

'You can be very dictatorial, Rosamund,' he said, a slight smile bringing some life into the sombre eyes.

'Oh, I know,' she said calmly. 'That was the gist of one of your earlier criticisms of me,' she added roguishly. 'I made too many decisions, you said. So it won't surprise you to learn that I've been over to Meronthorpe, and cleared your father's room. I hope I wasn't taking too much upon myself.'

He came over to her. His arms went around her and he pulled her to him fiercely. 'Thanks,' he said in a strangled voice. The one word touched her more poignantly than any gracious speech could have done. Averting her face, she moved gently away and went into the kitchen. He was making things very hard for her, and she mustn't lose sight of her resolution. She would be glad when things got back to normal again and Nick reverted to his true self. She mustn't fall into the trap of allowing the present situation to sway her judgement.

Ewan was back in time for the funeral, and the little church was crowded. Some of the mourners came from as far away as Scotland and Cornwall, and needed accommodation for the night, so Roz and Nick moved into Meronthorpe temporarily. It made things easier all round, especially for Nick, who had so many loose ends to tie up. But afterwards, as each day passed, he seemed more able to take up the reins, and a week after the funeral he suggested that they dine out.

'I'd like that,' Roz said. 'I must admit to feeling a bit claustrophobic.'

'Me, too. Strange how one's own life takes over again. I suppose it's a good thing,' Nick said thoughtfully.

'And it's what Rolfe would have wanted,' Roz told him gently.

But she didn't enjoy the evening, despite the delicious food which she could only pick at, and Nick's efforts to make the occasion a success. She had been pleased to be busy during the past days, but now there was nothing more to be done. They had come to the end. Without a doubt Nick would soon pick up the threads again, she thought cynically, toying with her *crêpe Suzette*; as for herself, she would devote all her energies to building up her business and preparing for the baby. She wondered if Nick and Gabriella had been in touch during the last few days. The photograph was still in her handbag. She had deliberately kept it as a reminder of her intentions when she felt herself in danger of weakening—like tonight.

Meronthorpe was quiet when they got back. Paul was out and the servants had gone to bed. A log fire was dying down when Roz followed Nick into the drawing-room, knowing that he would offer her a nightcap before they went to their separate rooms. Tonight she must tell him; she could no longer go on pretending.

He seemed to sense that she had something on her mind, for when he handed her a drink he said mildly, 'You took nervous, Rosamund. What have you been up to?'

But her courage failed her and when she said lamely, 'Why...nothing,' he changed the subject.

'How would you feel about living here at Meronthorpe? I know how you love Grey Garth, but this is my inheritance, and it's only right that I take up my place here.'

'Yes.' She nodded vehemently. 'Of course you must. But I...' She put down her glass and stood up uncertainly, then she moved over to a cabinet of ivories. 'Nick, I'm going back to Grey Garth. As you say, this is your rightful place now...' Her voice died, and her heart began to thud alarmingly. I've said it now, she told herself. It's over and done with. Another decision. I've said it clumsily, but he knows now. She held her breath, waiting for his answer, then when he didn't speak she said on a note of desperation, 'Nick? Did you hear? I'm——'

'Yes.' His voice seemed to re-echo around the room. 'Oh, yes, I heard. You're going back to Grey Garth and I'm staying here. You're telling me that it's over. You and I are finished.' His voice hardened suddenly into the tones which she knew so well. Incisive, authoritative. 'As I once remarked, you certainly choose your moments.'

Her face was mask-like in the reflecting glass of the cabinet. She saw herself nod as if she were watching someone else. Then she turned to face him. 'I'm sorry, but it's better this way, and I can't put off telling you any longer.'

'I see.' He was watching her closely, his eyes narrowed. 'So this has been on your mind for some time? And I assume that only the situation with my father prevented your telling me earlier?'

'Something like that, yes.'

'Then I should be grateful for your sensitivity, my dear,' he said bitingly.

'Don't be angry. Our marriage is no good for either of us.'

'You're the sole judge of that, of course.' She flinched from his heavy sarcasm.

'All right, then, our marriage is no good for *me*! Is that better?' She bit her lip when he didn't answer, the silence pressing against her eardrums like an ache. 'I'm sorry about the—the money and Ewan and the whole——'

'To hell with the money!' he roared. 'What the devil are you doing, Rosamund? You just don't confront a husband with the news that you're leaving him as if it were of no more consequence than the weather, for pity's sake! And then start talking about money!'

'Look,' she implored, trying to steady her quivering voice, 'and listen to me, *please*! I knew from—the beginning that it wouldn't work, but... And that's another thing,' she said wildly, going off at a tangent. 'You lied about that. You told me that the money was a loan to Ewan.' Too late, she remembered that she had betrayed Ewan's confidence, but somehow that didn't seem to matter now.

'Oh, so you know about that, do you?' he said grimly. 'Yes, all right, I lied—out of consideration for your pride. You seem to have overlooked something, Rosamund: I *knew* you, or I *thought* I did, although I must say you've changed a bit since those days. But just supposing I had told you that I was making over a substantial amount of money as a *gift*, would you have accepted?' He laughed mirthlessly. 'Of course you wouldn't! But I figured that if I put it to you on a businesslike basis, there was a chance.'

For a moment Roz was quiet. He knows me all right, she thought. 'Why did you do it?' she said dully at last. 'I was crazy to accept, and I knew it at the time, but there seemed no other way out. And I thought—hoped— that we might ... manage things better. Instead, we ...' She shrugged. 'But we'll pay you back, Ewan and I, and——'

With one lithe movement he was in front of her. Those familiar patches bleached the corners of his mouth, and his eyebrows were knotted with fury. 'For heaven's sake,' he thundered, 'will you stop talking of money? That has nothing to do with anything. You say you're leaving me, and I'm asking you *why*.' His fingers bit into her upper arms, pinioning them to her sides. 'Damn it, I have a right to know.' He glared down at her, his eyes like those of some magnificent jungle cat.

The golden glints in his eyes ignited her angry sense of betrayal. Deliberately she had hoped to conduct this scene in a controlled, low-key manner, but if anyone was entitled to be angry, surely it was herself! She jerked herself away from him, her eyes snapping. 'A right?' she breathed. '*You* speak of—*rights*? Don't I have rights, too? And I'm exercising one of them now. I'm opting out, Nick. And so far as I can see, *you* forfeited your rights at the convention.'

'The—*convention*? What the hell are you talking about, Rosamund? *You* walked out on *me*, remember? You suddenly decided in that delightful, quixotic way of yours, that you had had enough. So you left. And I came home to find you being oh, so sociable with the Rivers bloke. That's the way I see it, and that's the way it *was*.'

A log fell in the hearth and the noise made her jump. The room seemed to throb with self-generating fury that made a mockery of the gentle, pastel shades, the pleasant water-colours and the muted chintzes.

'You can forget Coran Rivers,' she snapped. 'He was incidental.' She lifted her head, tilting her chin and regarding Nick coldly in a sidelong, assessing gaze. 'Didn't it occur to you,' she asked softly, 'to ask yourself just *why* I had had enough?'

'Of course it did. And you already know the conclusion I drew. Lovemaking has the effect of making you want to take flight. One of your more immature little quirks,' he went on icily, ignoring her gasp of rage. 'But we went into that the night I came home, and I see no point in re-hashing it.'

Roz shot him a pitying glance. 'It must be wonderful to shrug off responsibility as easily as that,' she said in mock-admiration. She crossed over to a chair and sat down. Inwardly she felt shaky and insecure, but she swallowed and made herself speak calmly. 'Do you mean to tell me,' she asked carefully, 'that the possibility hadn't entered your head that I realised what you were up to?'

'Up to?' He loomed over her frowning, 'Perhaps you would clarify that. You appear to know something that I don't.'

Roz hesitated for a second. He was certainly putting up a good bluff. If she didn't know better, she might even be misled into thinking she had made a mistake. 'I'm speaking of—Gabriella, of course,' She had to wrench the name from that inner mass of misery that had built up. 'You couldn't wait to be alone with her that morning, could you? The morning after—after we—slept together. I won't use your term—*lovemaking*; you've debased it.' Why, oh, why did she have to go through all this again? After all, surely Nick must have realised that there was little future in remaining married to each other.

He was still frowning, but there was uncertainty, too, in the way he watched her. Then his brief, harsh laugh broke the silence. 'I'm not believing this,' he breathed. 'Do you mean to say that you actually thought that Gabriella and I were... For heaven's sake, Rosamund, she's an old friend!'

'And friendship comes in all shapes and sizes? Nick, I'm not blind. I know she's an *old friend*. You were with her on the night of my birthday almost two and a half years ago to the date.' Despite herself, her voice had sunk to little more than a bitter whisper, and the words were difficult to speak. She turned her face away from his imprisoning gaze and reached into her handbag. 'This is yours,' she mumbled, 'complete with the inscription on the back. I found it—in one of your books.'

Nick barely glanced at the photograph which shook in her hand, and after a moment she dropped it on to the small round table beside her. Nick's eyes came back to her thoughtfully. 'I think I'm beginning to understand,' he said quietly.

'Good. So perhaps you'll also understand why I have no intention of prolonging this so-called marriage.' She went over to a table against the wall. As she poured herself a drink, the decanter chattered against the glass. She needed something to hold on to, something to do. She had made the right decision; how could anyone condemn a child to a life so turbulent and insecure, so fraught with confrontation and bitterness? She took a sip and shuddered, feeling her throat protest. 'So I'm setting myself free, Nick,' she resumed. 'And you, too. You ought to be grateful. After all,' she went on, with a random sweeping gesture of her arm, 'all this— Meronthorpe with its acres and its farms—is yours now. And from the terms of Rolfe's will, I gather that you're a very wealthy man. *Old* money, too,' she mocked. 'Perhaps now Gabriella will be prepared to share it all with you. Maybe if you speak to her nicely she'll agree to getting a divorce and you'll both live—live—happily ever...' Her voice died. She sat down suddenly, closing her eyes.

Under his breath, Nick swore. He came across to her and took the glass out of her hand, banging it down so that some of the brandy spilled and lay like a fat tear on the highly polished surface of the table.

'You don't need that,' he barked. 'You sound fuddled enough already.'

'Don't treat me like a half-wit,' she stormed. 'I——'

'Why not, when you persist in behaving like one? Now listen, and listen carefully,' he gritted. 'Gabriella is a widow. A *widow*—got that? Good. So if I had wanted to marry her and she was willing, we could have tied the knot some time ago. Tell me, Rosamund, am I making sense?'

'You might be,' she muttered, 'if you were telling the truth. But I happened to hear one of the women at the convention say how well Gabriella has done for herself. And I saw her wedding ring, you know...'

'There's no law against a widow wearing her ring, is there? And that woman, whoever she was, was right; Gabriella *has* done well for herself—*professionally*. And all credit is due to her. After her husband died just over two years ago, she picked herself up and—'

'But...this photograph?' Roz whispered, her eyes wide and uncomprehending. It wasn't possible that she could be mistaken...was it?

'Her husband, Max, was a great friend of mine,' Nick said tersely. 'We all took a business trip to Majorca one year, the summer before he died. *I* took that snap of Gabriella, and if you care to look more closely you'll see Max in the background.'

'But at the convention——'

Nick made an exclamation of impatience. 'All right, so you saw me with Gabriella. So what? She wanted my advice on a point she wished to raise at one of the discussions. We had to snatch a moment when we could.' He looked down at Roz contemptuously. 'Should I have asked your permission?'

Roz felt something inside her wizen as the enormity of her mistake struck her forcibly. She looked up at Nick and made a little groping movement of appeal.

But his face had settled into sombre lines, and there were no golden lights in his eyes, only a brooding, reflective gaze. 'What a fool you are, Rosamund,' he said at length, and she flinched from the raw disdain in his tone. 'Why on earth didn't you simply ask me about Gabriella? Or even confront me with your suspicions? Instead you had to jump to the wrong conclusion and twist it right out of perspective, using it to feed your hatred of me. You're right about one thing, though: our marriage could never work!'

'I—I didn't—hate you,' she whispered.

'No? Well, then, you gave a hell of a good imitation at times. And *this* was the reason! A pure fabrication of your own making which you chose to regard as the truth!'

He turned and walked away from her to stand in front of the fire, his back towards her, but from the set of his shoulders she recognised his anger, and she felt it reaching her in waves that made her want to hide.

At last she said in a subdued voice, 'You said that Gabriella's husband died just over two years ago. That must have been soon after my birthday.' She swallowed. 'You cancelled our date, remember? You had told me that you were in Birmingham on business. You telephoned me from Birmingham. Yet I saw you that evening, only a couple of miles away from *here*. You were sitting in the car park of the Packhorse. And Gabriella was with you. Can you wonder that I didn't trust you after that?'

Nick turned then and went blindly to his chair, dropping down and putting his head into his hands, his long fingers raking the thick, tawny hair into disarray. When he looked up his face was haggard. 'I see,' he said heavily. 'And that's when it began, is it? And ever since then you've been nursing your suspicions, poisoning yourself with them? So the day after you saw me with Gabriella, you went off to Chester after handing me a bundle of lies about not wanting a serious relationship. What a coward you are, Rosamund!' His voice flicked like a whip. 'Just to put the record straight, not that it really matters now, but... I *did* go to Birmingham, and I had every intention of being back to take you out to dinner. I had planned—something special. But Gabriella was at the meeting in Birmingham, deputising for Max. She knew that he was going to die; most of the time he didn't recognise her. She had to talk to someone, and who better than me? She was—understandably—distraught. So I brought her back to Meronthorpe for the night. On the way back we stopped at a hotel for tea. It was a small place, with a telephone in the foyer. I rang you from there. Gabriella was right beside me and I couldn't go into all the details then. You simply assumed that I phoned from Birmingham. I would have given you the full story the following day, but you didn't give me the chance. You couldn't wait to get away!' He stopped, then looked across at her with the face of a stranger. 'Didn't you trust me at all?'

Roz closed her eyes, not wanting to read what she saw in his face. 'How could I? There was so much in your past that made a mockery of—of——'

'Go on,' he said mercilessly. 'Of what?'

'Of the way I—felt about you, damn it!' She was almost crying now, and she bent her head to stare down at her hands twisting together in her lap. She should have felt gladness that Nick's friendship with Gabriella was innocent, but instead she was filled with a searing sense of shame that she had been so ready to misjudge him. At last she got up. 'I'm going home,' she said dully. 'I can't talk—think—any more tonight.' She took a deep breath that sounded like a sob.

'I'll drive you, then.'

In the car he was silent. No words were sufficient to bridge the abyss that yawned between them. When she got out of the car at Grey Garth, she didn't even say goodnight.

Ewan was home. As Roz went through the hall, she could see that there was a light in the kitchen, and she heard him slam the cutlery drawer. She couldn't face anyone tonight. Instead, she called, 'I'm back, Ewan. I'm going straight up. Nick's staying at Meronthorpe.'

'Sleep well,' he shouted. He sounded bright and happy. Would she ever sound that way again? she wondered. She was free now to embark on that brave new self-reliant life she had promised herself and the baby. But there was no comfort in the thought, no relief that she had put her marriage behind her. Through her hideous suspicions and lack of faith she had lost Nick irrevocably.

The sleeping-tablet she took had its desired effect, but she awoke just before six. The lively birdsong outside her window made a sharp contrast to her own drugged and lifeless movements. She would make herself a pot of tea and bring it up, then perhaps she might sleep again. In her present state the thought of the day ahead with its small routine demands defeated her.

She hadn't heard Ewan moving about, and she was already in the kitchen before she saw him. Too late to escape now. 'Good *morning*!' he exclaimed breezily, then he saw her face. 'Something's wrong?' he said quickly. 'Sit down. I'll make your tea.'

Roz's mirror had mercilessly shown her the darkly shadowed eyes, the pallor of her face, and the drooping mouth. She opened her eyes wide, forcing herself to stare out over the garden to keep back the tears which Ewan's perception had awoken. 'Here,' he said, putting down a big mug. 'Drink it up. You'll soon feel better. You've had a rough time lately. I expect it's reaction setting in.'

Roz puckered her trembling mouth and took a short, scalding sip. 'It's—not that, Ewan,' she said in a dead voice. 'You might as well know... Nick and I have finished. Split up.'

'*No!* But you seemed so ——' His forehead creased in disbelief.

'Happy? That was just a sham. Our marriage never worked. Really, it didn't have much chance when you consider just why it——' She bit off the words hurriedly, aghast at how near she had come to letting Ewan see his own involvement in the whole miserable mess. 'It was my fault,' she went on painfully. 'I thought Nick was having an affair with—someone. Well, that's not so unbelievable, is it?' she went on, a note of self-defence

creeping into her voice. 'I mean, considering his reputation...' Then the tears won.

Ewan let her cry for a while as he quietly prepared his
breakfast. When finally she looked up, reaching blindly
for the mug, he passed her a handkerchief. 'I was under
the impression,' he began carefully, 'that when you
started seeing Nick again you had decided that all the
gossip about him was simply—just gossip.'

Roz didn't answer. That pretence had been necessary
in order to convince Ewan that she was happy about the
marriage.

Ewan stirred his coffee thoughtfully. 'And no doubt
some of it was,' he continued. 'Like that tale of the police
being called in to a party at Meronthorpe. Oddly enough,
Paul mentioned that affair a few weeks ago. It seems
that they had gatecrashers, a motorbike gang, riding all
over the lawns and through the flowerbeds. The old man
was about to threaten them with his shotgun. You can
imagine that, can't you? Anyway, Nick called the police
but didn't press charges.'

Roz gave a weary shrug. What did it matter now? It
was too late. 'There were other things,' she said list-
lessly. 'The very first time I met Nick at Ilona's party,
I overheard two girls talking. Apparently Nick was in
the throes of an affair with a married woman—Melody
someone-or-other...'

'Hargreaves,' Ewan said succinctly.

'You know her?' Roz looked up.

'I know *of* her,' Ewan corrected. 'She's a man-eater,
one of those women who seize upon a bloke's most innocent statement, then tell everyone he's mad about
them. I can't really see Nick having any...' He grimaced, shaking his head.

'Well, it doesn't matter now, does it?' Roz whispered.

'So you thought he was carrying on an affair? It must
have knocked him for six to find that you chose to believe all that old talk,' Ewan said at last.

Roz nodded silently. 'And, of course, he *wasn't* having an affair. Oh, Ewan, I've made a hopeless mess of things.'

Ewan buttered toast slowly, then he said thoughtfully, 'I once thought things were hopeless, too. And I fed that hopelessness by not trying to—to sort myself out. And you know what the outcome of that was. But now I've got a grip on life again. And, of course, I've met Denny. You'll like her. But what I'm really trying to say, Roz, is that few things are actually hopeless. OK, you've misjudged Nick, so why don't you go and see him again? Apologise. Tell him how—uncertain of him you really were, and that's why you misjudged him. But for heaven's sake don't brood about the place being miserable without at least trying to make amends. Simply convince him that you're sorry. After all, it must have been a great blow to him to learn that you gave such credence to idle gossip, letting it mislead you into thinking he was after another woman after only three months of marriage! I mean, I can imagine how I'd feel in his place.'

'Seeing him won't do any good,' Roz murmured miserably.

'Well, it won't do any harm either. After all, you've both had a night to sleep on things. Maybe it'll look different to him this morning. He's a good guy, Roz. You can't put paid to a marriage in one evening! And you mustn't accept the situation as being beyond repair. Where's that old fighting spirit?'

Roz managed a faint smile. 'Dormant, I think. Well, thanks for your counsel.' She looked at him affectionately. 'You sound full of confidence and energy,' she remarked wistfully.

'I am. I've discovered that very few things in life are one hundred per cent insurmountable. I've got to fly now. Go and see him. Or at least think about it. Will you?'

She nodded mutely. Maybe she would. Some time.

She poured more tea and took it upstairs. Perhaps she would be able to think more positively after she had slept again.

But sleep wouldn't come. The effects of the pill had worn off, and there had been a lot of sense in Ewan's advice. Suddenly she flung back the duvet. She showered quickly and made up her face carefully, satisfied to see that already the harrowed expression had left her eyes. She took a grey dress from her wardrobe, knotted a sliver of red silk scarf at the neck and ran downstairs, picking up the fashion doll on the way out.

As she drove, she dared not allow herself to think ahead or she might turn back, daunted by the memory of Nick's face, his scathing tone. Instead she hummed tunelessly to the radio, concentrating on the road ahead.

She drew up outside the portico of Meronthorpe and went straight in before her courage failed. The breakfast-room door was open, and Nick was sitting at the table, drinking black coffee and reading his mail.

As she went in, he rose formally. 'Oh, good morning, Rosamund. I expect you've come for your clothes.'

'Yes ... No.' Her heart plunged at the arctic tone, but she stumbled on. 'I want to—talk,' she whispered.

Slowly he refolded a letter and slid it back into its envelope. 'I think,' he said distantly, 'you said enough last night.' He picked up a paper-knife and slit another envelope.

She watched him for a moment silently, hopelessly. Then she said, almost to herself, 'Or—not enough.' She half turned to go, and remembered the doll. She faced him again, taking it out of her bag. 'I think,' she whispered, the words catching on a sob, 'that you should keep this. It meant a great deal to—your mother. You should ask Miss Berridge to tell you about... And I think it also pleased Rolfe during the last...' The constriction of her throat cut off her words and blindly she went towards the door.

'Wait,' Nick's voice rapped out. 'Very well, I'll listen. We'd better go into the drawing-room.' Then, a few minutes later, as they faced each other across the hearth, he said, 'Well? What is it you want to say?'

'Just that—I'm sorry.' Roz looked up at him, her eyes enormous with unshed tears. 'I've been so stupid... Will you—can you—forgive me? And won't you even try to understand how I felt?'

'Might it not be better to forget the whole thing?' Nick said tautly after a moment.

'I—don't want to forget—all of it,' Roz breathed. 'Some of it I'll *never* forget. There were...' She bit her lip. 'There were happy moments, too. The happiest moments of my life.' She swallowed. 'But then, underlying them was always——'

'Your mistrust of me,' he said baldly.

'Yes. That's why I'm apologising.'

For a moment he didn't speak, and Roz glanced up at him, seeing now the strain on his face, the rigidly controlled features which gave no indication of his emotions. Then he said thoughtfully, 'You said something last night about my behaviour making a mockery of the way you felt.' He was watching her steadily. 'How *did* you feel, Rosamund?'

'I *loved* you! You must have known that.' She felt the treacherous sobs jerk at her mouth, distorting her words, and she turned her head away so that he shouldn't see her face. 'I always loved you,' she said desperately, 'but—if I'm honest, I have to say that it was—against my better judgement.'

He nodded indifferently. 'So we're back to my wild reputation, I suppose?' He got up and went to stand at the window, his hands in his pockets. Roz guessed that his fists were tightly clenched. 'Well, perhaps I earned it in part. Heaven knows, I wasn't a monk. And I didn't reach the age of thirty-four in a world entirely devoid of women. And some of them I even loved—a little. Then I met you. And it was important, and it's been important ever since—even during the two years when we didn't meet. But that doesn't mean to say that I didn't have the odd little fling. You see? I, too, am being absolutely honest with you.'

Mutely she nodded, getting up to pace the room, beating her fists together. 'But try to understand how I felt,' she implored. 'Nick Martel, the high-flyer, the man to whom all gifts were given—or so it seemed. How could I be *sure*? I—*thought* at the time that you—loved me, but I had to question it. Can't you see? I felt—insecure. One of the wives at the convention mentioned—country mice——'

'And that's how you saw yourself?' He spun round to stare at her. 'Oh, Rosamund, Rosamund, if only you hadn't taken off for Chester that day, I *would* have convinced you.'

Impatiently she dashed away a tear. 'I came to the conclusion that love was just a game to you. And I *did* see you kiss Gabriella in the Packhorse car park.'

'Yes, you probably did,' he said flatly. 'I don't remember, but it's possible that I did it out of a natural desire to comfort her. We only stopped at the Packhorse because she was shivering and there's always a big fire there. She needed a friend, that's all.' He gave a sigh. 'But I didn't kiss her in the way I have kissed you.'

Roz felt a quiver run through her as she remembered the bliss of his lips. 'I'm sorry,' she breathed again. 'But then I found a poem, and you had marked some lines about—about hair being twined in . . . waterfalls . . .' She compressed her lips to gain a moment's self-control. 'And after that,' she went on at last, dully, 'I saw that you had kept a photograph of Gabriella with her hair blowing. So—so . . .'

'You thought I associated Gabriella's hair with those lines?' he finished. He came across to her and took her hand, leading her to the sofa, and drawing her down beside him. 'It was *your* hair, Rosamund.' He picked up a strand and rubbed it gently between finger and thumb. 'You wore it longer and wilder in those days. I marked those lines soon after we parted. They described exactly how I felt. You were all around me, yet you had gone.'

She leaned her head against his arm, unable to speak.

'Then, when Ewan got into a mess, I saw it as an opportunity to get you back. I had to be so careful; you didn't like—involvements. You were too much of a free spirit; at least, that's what you had me believing.' Restlessly he got up, moving away, and she felt an acute sense of loss. 'I *did* sympathise with Ewan, you know. After all, I, too, had lost the girl I loved. But I was so angry with him for putting you through it, and I gave him a hard time that night. And yet, I figured, if it gave me a chance to get you back into my life again, then we might make it in the end.'

He turned, and she saw self-mockery in his smile. 'And I won't deny there was a touch of revenge about it. Hell, Rosamund, you had made me suffer. I had planned to ask you to marry me on your twenty-fourth birthday. You swept all that away. I wanted to hurt you, Rosamund.'

'Well,' she sighed, 'you achieved that, anyway.' They seemed to have said everything now. She had apologised, and that was what she had come here to do. But it hadn't solved anything; the agony must abate, she told herself helplessly. No one can endure this amount of pain for ever. He had loved her once, but she hadn't trusted him. And now it was too late for anything except understanding. She stood up to leave.

'No, wait. Wait a moment,' he said sharply, and went out of the room.

Roz sat staring blankly about her, seeing nothing. What a mess she had made of it all, deliberately cancelling out the moments of happiness they had shared, jeopardising the moments they *would* share... And now there was the baby, whose right to a father she had denied through her stupidity.

She glanced round as Nick came back. He was holding a small velvet box. 'This was meant for you,' he said. 'You might as well have it now. Give me your hand. No, the other one.'

She held out her left hand, palm down, and he put his own hand beneath. And suddenly it was all there again in the touch of palm against palm. A gasp tore through her as a sudden heat blazed in her veins, and her heart leaped giddily as the conflagration grew inside her. It was still there—that incredible, wonderful feeling she had known that morning in the attic among the old toys. She stared up at Nick, her eyes enormous, hardly daring to search... Then she saw from his face that he felt it, too.

Without speaking, he slid off her diamond solitaire engagement ring and dropped it in his pocket. From the little box he took another ring, antique, with a half-hoop of stones, the initial of each spelling the word *dearest*: diamond, emerald, amethyst, ruby, emerald, sapphire, topaz. A ring infinitely more personal than the sparkling, conventional solitaire.

'Your twenty-fourth birthday present,' he said quietly. 'Just two and a half years late. But not *too* late.'

The little velvet box made a soft thud as it hit the carpet and his arms went round her, gathering her closely to himself. She felt the strength of his body, the pressure of his chest and thighs against hers as his lips sought hers, half open in a sigh of wonder. The sudden flicker of his tongue fed the flame of longing that leapt in her, and her hands reached up to cradle his jaw, each finger sensuously celebrating the warm golden skin. He untied the red silk scarf, and it fluttered down to join the blue velvet box. He laid his lips against her throat, and the rapid beating of her pulse answered the kiss.

At last he lifted his head, his eyes darkened with desire. 'There's only one place to go on from here,' he said huskily, 'and that's forward. Rosamund?' It was an offer she didn't have to examine any more. She gave a tiny, inarticulate nod.

He swung her off her feet and carried her towards the stairs, and she had a last struggling moment of sanity. 'What about—the maids?' she whispered.

'I'm a gambling man, darling,' he said. 'Our marriage was one big gamble. When I went to get your ring, I took a chance and gave them the rest of the day off.'

Beneath her cheek she felt the throb of his heart like a compelling, intoxicating instrument. 'We have hours ahead of us,' he said. 'Hours, days, years...'

Time enough, Roz thought, as he laid her upon the bed, time to show him how much I love him. Time to tell him about the baby. But not yet. This is our moment. And we've both waited so long.

With her heart in her eyes and her lips curving in soft invitation, she put out her arms and drew him down beside her.

VOWS   *LaVyrle Spencer*   £2.99

When high-spirited Emily meets her father's new business rival, Tom, sparks fly, and create a blend of pride and passion in this compelling and memorable novel.

LOTUS MOON   *Janice Kaiser*   £2.99

This novel vividly captures the futility of the Vietnam War and the legacy it left. Haunting memories of the beautiful Lotus Moon fuel Buck Michael's dangerous obsession, which only Amanda Parr can help overcome.

SECOND TIME LUCKY   *Eleanor Woods*   £2.75

Danielle has been married twice. Now, as a young, beautiful widow, can she back-track to the first husband whose life she left in ruins with her eternal quest for entertainment and the high life?

These three new titles will be out in bookshops from September 1989.

W●RLDWIDE

Experience the thrill of 4 Mills & Boon Romances

FREE BOOKS FOR YOU

Enjoy all the heartwarming emotions of true love.
The dawning of a passion too great for you to control. The
uncertainties and the heartbreak. And then, when it seems
almost too late - the ecstasy that knows no bounds!

Now you can enjoy four captivating Romances as a **free** gift
from Mills & Boon, plus
the chance to have
6 Romances delivered
to your door every
single month.

Turn the page for details of 2 extra free gifts, and how to apply

An irresistible offer from Mills & Boon

Here's a personal invitation from Mills & Boon to become a regular reader of Romance. And to welcome you, we'd like you to have four books, an enchanting pair of glass oyster dishes and a special MYSTERY GIFT.

Then each month you could look forward to receiving 6 more brand – new Romances, delivered to your door, post and packing **free**. Plus our newsletter featuring author news, competitions and special offers.

This invitation comes with no strings attached. You can stop or suspend your subscription at any time, and still keep your **free** books and gifts.

It's so easy. Send no money now. Simply fill in the coupon below at once and post it to -

Reader Service, FREEPOST, P.O Box 236, Croydon, Surrey. CR9 9EL

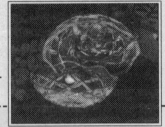

✂ - - - - - - - - - - *No stamp required* - - - - - - - -

YES! Please rush me my 4 Free Romances and 2 FREE gifts!

Please also reserve me a Reader Service Subscription. If I decide to subscribe, I can look forward to receiving 6 brand new Romances each month, for just £8.10 delivered direct to my door. Post and packing is **free**. If I choose not to subscribe I shall write to you within 10 days - I can keep the books and gifts whatever I decide. I can cancel or suspend my subscription at any time.
I am over18.

EP61R

NAME —————————————————————————————

ADDRESS ———————————————————————————

——————————————————————————————————

—————————————————— *POSTCODE* ———————————

SIGNATURE ————————————————————————————